GASH

EVERNIGHT PUBLISHING ®

www.evernightpublishing.com

GASH

DEDICATION

I want to thank all of my wonderful readers for their patience. I know Gash has taken some time but I needed for him to be right. A big thank you to the wonderful Karyn White, my editor, who has helped me to shape every single Skull book. Also, thank you to Evernight for giving my MC a home.

You're all amazing and supportive.

GASH

GASH

The Skulls, 13

Sam Crescent

Copyright © 2016

Chapter One

Charlotte Bilson placed her hand at her throat as she glanced across the table at a fuming Gash. He looked bigger than she imagined, and she placed her hand around her neck, just to make sure everything was fine with her. Yep, her neck was still in place, which was a relief. Coming home to find Gash inside her apartment, and not only that, to have him attack her, hadn't exactly been the kind of welcome she wanted.

"Did you have to attack me like that?" she asked.

"I didn't attack you."

She raised a brow, but didn't actually say anything to him to refute him. It had been years since she last saw him. Age had done wonders for him, and yet it hadn't at the same time. He was harder than she remembered, colder too. There were times where she recalled him always smiling, always laughing. Now, the man she once knew was gone, dead almost. He constantly wore a frown, and he was staring at her as if he'd like to kill her. She'd been in his company a matter of minutes, and yet she saw the change inside him, the darkness.

He does want to kill you.

"Do you know what the word attack actually means?"

"You're alive."

"That has nothing to do with the word attack. Seriously, get a dictionary!"

He stared at her with his cold eyes. "Do you really think you should be testing me right now?"

"I don't give a fuck. You come into my place, attack me, and now you want me to treat you like what? Some fucking person I know?" She hadn't unloaded her anger in over five years. It had been two years since Gash's release from prison, and he had gone down for five years before that. Seven complete years of living without a damn care in the world. Her life meant shit to her, quite literally. She didn't care.

"Tell me where Rebecca Charleston is," he said, moving from his position at the table. He grabbed a chair, turned it, and sat down so that he was leaning on the back of the chair.

She started to laugh. "I don't know where she is."

"You said you're going to help me."

"I promised to help you, Gash. I didn't tell you that I knew where Rebecca was. I said I'd take out, but I don't know where she is. I don't know where either of them are. I figured you'd know. You came to me, not the other way around," she said.

"Why did you think that?"

"You found me." She shrugged. "I have to say I'm surprised."

"You think after serving five years for a rape and murder that I didn't commit, I'd leave you alone." He reached out, tucking some hair behind her ear, startling her.

"What are you doing?" she asked, jerking away.

"Nothing."

Shaking her head, she went to stand up, but Gash grabbed her arm. She didn't want him to be touching her. The last thing she wanted was his tenderness. Gash hadn't come back into her life with sweet words. He'd come with threats.

"I didn't give you permission to stand up, so sit the fuck down!"

Yanking her arm away from him, she lowered back down in her chair. She didn't like how she felt just from the touch of his fingers on her arm. Did he remember their time together at all? One night where he'd taken her virginity, blown her world, and he didn't have any recollection. Should she be embarrassed that she wasn't that memorable?

God, she'd stopped thinking about all of this shit since she got out of a fucking mental ward, and now he was back, making her relive it all again.

Not all of it. Gash wasn't responsible for what that bastard, Jeff Wright, did to her.

Forget about it. Stop thinking about what happened, and focus on what is going on now.

"Will you stop manhandling me?" She cradled her arm against her chest. *I'm not going to be affected by him. He means nothing to me, and he clearly doesn't know what I've lost.*

"What's your problem?"

"You're my problem. You storm into my apartment, attack me, and now you're ordering me around. I'm not a damn child, so stop yelling at me." Her heart was pounding. This was not the kind of reunion she ever imagined having with Gash. She didn't imagine hearts and flowers, but she didn't imagine this, accusations, threats. They had been friends once. Didn't that account for something? Her throat was a little sore from where he'd gripped her around the neck.

They were not getting anywhere at the moment. They were both just yelling at each other, and that didn't help anyone. Violence never worked, yet that was what they both wanted, to kill their enemies.

Sitting back in her chair, she stared past his shoulder. The memories were starting to invade once again. "I had nothing to do with what happened to you. If you remember I went away because of work with my boss. I had to go to England. When I came back a month later, you were awaiting a date for the trial, and they wouldn't give you bail." By the time the trial would have happened, she wouldn't have been considered a reliable source as she already had a permanent place in a mental ward.

"I'm about to ask you a question, and I want you to answer me clearly. Did my lawyer get in touch with you?" Gash asked.

"Your lawyer?"

"Yes."

"No. I wasn't contacted by any lawyer."

"I fucking knew it."

It had been strange to her at the time as well. No lawyer had been in touch with her, and she'd only heard about it on the news as she was coming out of the airport. She didn't have time to tell her story. There had been a date for the trial, and she'd tried to get in touch with Gash's lawyer without success, and then it was too late. Jeff grabbed her, tore her world apart, and dumped her. After trying to take her own life, she'd been sent to a psychiatric hospital where she'd spent the next five years. Since getting out she had tried to find Rebecca and

Jeff, losing lots of money in her own search to find the people who'd ruined her life. She didn't have the right resources to find the two people who had ruined her life. Charlotte had to finally stop trying to hunt for ghosts.

Gash rubbed his temple. "I've spent a great deal of time thinking about this."

"When you first got sentenced, I was out of the country. I'd gotten a promotion, and I was on my way back. When I got back home, before your trial, I, erm, I got sick, and I couldn't help you, no matter what." Charlotte wasn't about to tell him what happened when she got back. She wasn't ready to delve into that shit again.

"I get that."

She shook her head and stood. "If you don't mind, I want a drink." She stormed into her kitchen, and as she filled the kettle, she noticed that her hands were shaking. Taking a deep breath, she moved from the kitchen sink, to the counter, and turned on the kettle. She had to keep control over her emotions. The last thing she needed right now was to lose herself again. She'd been doing so well right now.

I can do this.

Can you do this?

The father of your child is sitting at your pathetic excuse for a table.

You didn't have a child.

They destroyed that.

The very thoughts made her eyes fill with tears, and she tried to wipe them away.

It's in the past. I can't change the past.

Breathe in, breathe out.

It's good to live.

She kept speaking the words her therapist advised her to do. She wasn't about to waste years of therapy.

"Are you okay?" Gash asked, startling her. He stood right behind her. He gripped her waist, and she tensed up, jerking out of his hold.

"Don't."

"I don't recall you being this jumpy."

"How do you remember anything about me?" she asked.

"We spent a great deal of time together, Charlotte. Don't try to pretend that it didn't mean anything."

Slamming the cup down on the counter, she spun around to face him. This guy was giving her whiplash, and she was so damn tired of him, and tired of the past invading her present. "How can you say that? How can you say that we spent time together, and yet, you come in here, threatening me?" She shook her head. "I don't know anything about Rebecca and Jeff. I've been on my own for a long time."

"What happened to you?" he asked.

"What?"

"You're different. I remember a time when you had an easy smile, and were more than happy to talk with me. Now, you're treating me like you don't know me."

"It has been seven years, Gash. Do you have any idea what happens in seven years? People change. I'm not the same woman you knew, and you're not the same guy."

"I am."

"No. The guy I knew wouldn't have shoved me up against the wall with his hand wrapped around my neck. Neither of us are the same, and you need to realize that it's not going to fall back into old times."

Gash stared into her eyes, and she forced herself to stare right back at him. It was hard for her not to look away, but she wouldn't back down. He wasn't the same man, and she didn't trust him, not one bit.

"Did you and Rebecca have another friend?" he asked.

She frowned. "Huh?"

"I was wondering if you and Rebecca had another friend that visited you while I was here. I seem to recall a woman there, vaguely."

Charlotte turned back to finish her coffee. "No one else but you, me, Rebecca, and Jeff, oh, and the guy that turned up dead, who was just a boyfriend Rebecca had made sure she'd been seen with. Nothing else."

He touched her waist once again, leaning in close, invading her space. "Are you sure?"

"I'm more than sure, asshole." She pushed her butt out, making him take a step back. "There was no other woman, and Rebecca was screwing all of you." She took a seat back at the table, wrapping her fingers around the cup. "What's your plan? Are you going to threaten me to death, or do you actually have a plan for us to find the bastard and bitch who affected our lives?"

"You know nothing."

"What part of 'I've been looking for them for some time' didn't you understand?" She didn't know where her confidence was coming from. Gash terrified her, and so did their situation. She had agreed to kill the woman who had falsely accused Gash of raping her and murdering her boyfriend. Charlotte only knew half of what happened.

When she came back from her business trip, she'd been feeling off, and the only explanation had been the unprotected sex with Gash. She'd gotten a test, returned to her apartment, and had been overjoyed to learn she was pregnant. Jeff had been there, and he'd seen the test in her hands. What she hadn't realized at the time was the fact she'd touched her stomach, and said

Gash's name. Jeff had obviously had no doubt that she was carrying Gash's baby. In the few shorts seconds of happiness, she'd decided that, with her promotion, she'd finally get a place of her own, something that meant she didn't have to have a roommate. Charlotte had grown tired of all of the men around Rebecca, and she didn't want that kind of life for her baby. The moment she heard that Gash had been arrested, and a trial date was about to be set, she had been about to contact his lawyer in order to help him.

From the first moment she saw Gash, she'd been attracted to him. Every time she saw him, and got to know him, she'd fallen a little more in love with him. She was nothing like Rebecca, who'd been beautiful, slim, and completely experienced. Charlotte was not. They hadn't even been best friends, merely acquaintances who shared an apartment. Neither of them could afford a place, so they shared. Gash didn't know any of that. He thought they were best friends, when Charlotte hadn't liked Rebecca, not at all. She'd put up with her, nothing else. The promotion had been her ticket out of that life, but it had all gone to shit. Jeff had seen to that. Once she discovered that Gash was going down for not just rape but murder, she'd tried to help, and had failed. Instead, her very future had been ripped out of her. Jeff had been there, and had caught her taking the test. He'd asked who it was, and she shouldn't have told him. Gash didn't know everything that had been taken from her, and she hoped he never did. Gash didn't even know they had shared a night together, so he didn't need to know what else had happened. She'd tried to help him, really she had, and she had failed them both. It already hurt her too much to handle it. She doubted he would even believe it, let alone understand what she was going through.

****

Whizz didn't need to worry about Charlotte. She was fucking fire, and she was turning him on. Gash took a seat opposite her, and watched as she blew across the cup filled with coffee. His cock pressed against the front of his pants, and he stared into her eyes. She stared right back at him, and something ached in the back of his mind, like a memory trying to get out, but he couldn't reach it.

"I've not got a plan. Coming to you was my plan. However, I've got someone who can help us. Do you think you can help me locate them?" he asked. He didn't want to leave her alone. Charlotte was by his side now for the foreseeable future. Gash didn't know where these emotions were coming from, only that she was inspiring them. Her gaze was filled with so much pain that he found it hard to keep eye contact with her.

What had she been through? Charlotte had secrets, and he bet that Whizz knew some of them.

"I've been to your old apartment. It's a shithole now, and there's nothing there."

She blew out a breath, staring past his shoulder. "I've not been there in years."

"Is there anything you remember? Anything at all?"

"Rebecca was a popular girl. Before I left, she'd started making visits to some rich billionaire in the city. I don't know his name, but she told me he'd set up an apartment that he used when he was in town."

"What name?"

"It was in her name. The guy, I don't know who, didn't want to have a, er, track record or something. I figured he was just married, and didn't want any traces of him keeping a mistress." She shrugged. "I told her to tell you. She wouldn't. Rebecca said you were only after some good pussy, and you didn't care who she fucked."

"She got something right. Rebecca was a whore through and through. She didn't give a shit about anyone or anything." Gash stood, unable to look at Charlotte when he thought of Rebecca. He'd been young, and an asshole. What did he ever see in Rebecca? She'd been an easy fuck, and at the time he'd not been interested in anything but a good time.

He frowned, thinking about where their old apartment building was. It was a good hour from The Skulls clubhouse, and far enough away from Fort Wills. What the fuck had he been doing all those years ago? With the court case, prison, and the shit that had been going on since he got out, he wondered now what he'd been doing near Rebecca in the first place. Gash scrambled through his mind, and remembered. He'd been looking for his brother when he'd found Rebecca.

"Did I ever talk to you about The Skulls and shit back then?"

Charlotte frowned. "You never actually talked about anything with me. You were really quiet." Her cheeks heated. "You always had something else on your mind."

"What are you not telling me?"

"Nothing."

"You're in no position to hold something back—"

"The only time you were loud was when you were having sex with Rebecca. You didn't talk about anything. The only reason I knew you were part of The Skulls was because of your damn jacket. You didn't talk about them. Thinking about it, you were always so careful about what you did, in fact, talk about. You couldn't hide your leather cut." She pointed at the jacket he was wearing.

Gash had been looking for his brother who he

hadn't seen in some time. He'd never found him, so he assumed that he was dead. His real brothers were The Skulls. Gash made a mental note to talk to Tiny about it. Lash was the leader of The Skulls now, but Tiny was the leader back then and he'd been the one to give the orders.

"What's your plan?" she asked.

"You're coming back to the clubhouse with me. It's late right now, and I'm fucking tired. Tomorrow morning we'll head to the clubhouse where we're going to start our search for those two fuckers." He tilted his head to the side, and frowned when he heard a growling noise. "What the fuck was that?"

He noticed Charlotte went an even deeper shade of red.

"I'm hungry," she said.

"What?"

"I've not eaten since lunchtime. I'm starving, and I didn't exactly plan to get attacked tonight, and to starve."

"Anyone ever tell you that you've got a smart mouth?"

"It's not the only thing you've told me."

Gash frowned. "What else have I told you?" He couldn't help but wonder what else she meant by her words. There was clearly something there that she wanted to tell him, yet she didn't elaborate.

Charlotte shrugged. "I guess that is for you to find out." She shook her head, blowing out a breath. "I don't want to fight, okay? I actually just want to have some food. Being attacked in my own apartment has left me cranky."

He couldn't argue with that. He wanted her off balance and scared. Gash never claimed to be a nice guy. Years spent rotting in jail for a crime he didn't commit had chased away any kind of playfulness he possessed.

Fighting for his life had been his only companion, that and his need for revenge. Gash now had both within his grasp, but when he looked at Charlotte, the hatred wasn't there.

"Do you know how to cook?" he asked.

"Who do you think kept you fed when you visited?" she asked. "Rebecca couldn't cook to save her life. I was the one that cooked for you, me." She pointed to her chest, and beneath the pain, he saw the anger. Charlotte was angry at him. "It seems you make a habit of forgetting everything." She got to her feet, placing her hands on the table, and glared at him. "I'm going to make some food. Are you going to kill me for moving?"

"Sarcasm makes me horny, Charlotte. You keep on with that smart mouth, and I'll put it to better use."

"Funny, I thought rape was beneath you," she said.

"Believe me, babe, when I get you underneath me, you wouldn't be screaming rape. You'll be begging me for it." She clenched her teeth, and he couldn't resist getting to his feet, invading her space. "Would you like me to show you exactly how good it can be?"

She glared at him for another few seconds before storming past him, muttering under her breath.

"What?" he asked.

"Nothing. I'm going to make myself a chicken salad. You got a problem with that?"

"Do enough to feed me." Sitting back, he flicked open his phone, and dialed Whizz's number.

"What the fuck do you want?" Whizz asked as way of answering.

"That's no way to talk to your friend."

"You're not at the club, and right now you're not my friend." Whizz didn't agree with his need to go searching for Charlotte. "What kind of friend phones up late at night while I'm screwing my woman?"

Okay, maybe it had nothing to do with Charlotte.

"Am I cock blocking you?"

"No, you're pissing me off. What do you want? Lash has told me to take your calls no matter what. I'm simply obeying orders. What can I do to help? I'm just an all night fucking service." Whizz's voice was filled with sarcasm.

Gash laughed. He liked Whizz.

"You'll be pleased to know I'll be back at the club in a couple of days. I'll have Charlotte with me. Let the women know she's not a whore, but I've struck a deal with her. She's going to help me find the two people I want."

There was silence on the other end.

"You still there?"

"I'll help you. I want to talk to Charlotte alone," Whizz said.

"Seriously? What is your fucking deal?"

"That's the deal I'm going to make. You want me to find who you're looking for, I want to talk to Charlotte. Believe me when I say that I've got your best interests at heart. You just don't see it."

"Fine. It's not like there's going to be much else for her to do. How's the club?" Gash asked. Since getting out of prison he'd kept himself confined to the clubhouse and the town of Fort Wills.

"The same. There are days kids are running around, and other days it's silent other than the singles fucking. I don't spend all that much time there anymore. It's why I have a cell phone. I'm actually at home with my wife and kid." In the background he heard Lacey cursing.

"How is Sally?" Gash asked. He liked the young kid. Whizz and Lacey couldn't have kids, so they had adopted the younger teenager.

"She's doing great. It's a relief that she has settled down at school, and she's not even causing trouble. There's no interest in boys yet, but I think it helped that I took several of the brothers with me to drop her off. They have backed the fuck off."

Gash laughed. "It'll only be a matter of time before she starts causing trouble."

"I own a lot of knives and guns. Let the little dicks think they can get close to her. I'll handle each and every one of them."

"I'll leave you to it." Gash stared at the curve of Charlotte's back, and a memory that was distant of another back, a naked back, flashed through his mind. Blinking back the memories, he focused back on the call. "I've got to go."

Chapter Two

Charlotte chopped the ingredients for the salad, trying her hardest not to listen to him, or to pay any attention to him. They were going back to The Skulls clubhouse. She never had anything to do with the club seven years ago, and Gash wasn't the same man he used to be. Then again, she wasn't the same woman. A lot had happened over the years to change her, and there was no way she'd ever be that same carefree woman again.

He ended the call, and she heard him move away from the table. She kept on chopping even as he moved up behind her.

"Did you have any other friends when we were younger?" he asked.

He moved her hair off her shoulder, exposing her neck. His breath fanned across her ear, and she couldn't help but close her eyes. Gash was stirring feelings and memories inside her that he couldn't even remember. She recalled another night where he'd been like this, touching her, caressing her.

"Back away," she said, whispering the words. It was hard as the two different times seem to merge in the one. She fought it. Charlotte wasn't about to let herself be brought down by memories. They were *her* memories.

"You don't sound like you want me to move away." His hand gripped her hip while the other forced her to pause on chopping the salad. "Did you have a friend back then besides Rebecca?"

"I've told you before, Rebecca and I were roommates, that's all. There was no one else." Charlotte knew why he was asking, but she wouldn't tell him what happened between them. He'd only laugh in her face. She didn't know whether to laugh or cry. Gash wanted to believe there was someone else there rather than see that it was her all along. He didn't even suspect it could be her, and that fucking hurt.

"You feel so familiar, and you smell so damn good." He pressed his face against her neck, taking a deep breath.

She gasped out at the flood of arousal that he caused, taking her off guard. She was transported to another time. The only difference between then and now was the fact he didn't have the scent of alcohol on his breath. Last time, he'd been drinking, and at first, she had brushed him off. The biggest problem for her was the fact she had always had a crush on him, always. From the moment she first met him, she'd loved him. She had watched him with Rebecca, and even though there had been moments of jealousy, she never did anything about it. That night though, he'd been different. Yes, he'd been drunk, but she truly believed he had been himself. Gash had been sweet, nice, and tender, and he'd made her fall for him even more. He'd told her how beautiful she was, and how he couldn't stop looking at her.

Even though he'd been drunk, she'd been pulled into his words, and that had been her mistake, and she shouldn't have fallen for him.

"What do you want?" she asked.

"Why does this feel good?"

She closed her eyes, allowing herself a few seconds of enjoying his closeness when reality came back. He had attacked her. Gash had been more than ready to kill her, and she wasn't ready to give in to him. She pushed him back with her ass. "Give me some space. It's not very nice to invade my personal area."

Charlotte finished chopping the salad, tossing the ingredients together and giving it a quick dressing before serving. Gash hadn't moved away, but she ignored him.

The last thing she wanted to do was cave. She had only known him for a short time when he was screwing Rebecca. She'd never wanted to be one of those women that dropped her panties the moment a guy looked her way, but Gash, he'd been different. At least, she thought he'd been different.

Putting his plate on the table, she took a seat, opening the food magazine that she had been reading that morning when her life had seemed so normal. She tried her hardest to ignore him. When he sat down, and his knees grazed hers, she struggled not to tense up from the simplest contact.

"You've changed," he said.

Glancing up at him, she took a bite of her chicken, staring. "So have you. The last time I knew you, you wouldn't have snuck into my apartment with the intention of killing me."

"I can't argue with that."

Charlotte twirled her fork on the plate as she thought about her next question. "Why have you waited so long?"

"Long for what?"

"Looking for them? Looking for Rebecca and that … man." She couldn't bring herself to say his name. Charlotte never in all of her life considered herself a violent person When it came to *him* she wanted to witness his suffering, to be laughing in his face as he took his final breath. "It has been seven years."

"I was in prison for five of those."

I was in a mental hospital, trying to kill myself.

"What about the other two?"

Gash sat back, chewing his food. "The Skulls is my family. It's the only family that I recognize."

"You have more family?"

"A brother. I've not seen him in years. To be

honest, he's probably dead. He's the one I was looking for when I was looking for Rebecca."

"You don't care?"

"Like I said, my family is The Skulls."

"I never knew you had a brother." Charlotte found it hard that he didn't seem to care, but then she didn't know his brother. "Sorry."

"Don't be. Blood doesn't make family, Charlotte. Actions, loyalty, and love, that's what makes a family. The Skulls were going through some serious shit by the time I was released. Tiny, my club Prez, he asked me to not go looking. I didn't see a reason to bring more shit to the club. We're all in a good place right now, and so I'm looking. I want to end this."

"That's a long time to wait."

"I'm a patient guy."

Biting her lip, she rolled the chicken and bread around her plate. "What happens when we find them?"

"We kill them."

"Yes, we will." She couldn't look at him right now. Charlotte couldn't tell him that when he was on trial she had been in a psych ward, trying to kill herself at every opportunity. How could she have helped him when she'd been doped up on drugs to stop her from trying to slit her wrist? Her hunger disappeared, and she got to her feet, dumping the contents of her plate into the trash. She needed to do something with her hands, and to stop nearly telling Gash about what happened. He blamed her for not coming forward, and she blamed herself as well. If she'd not taken that damn promotion, she'd have been here when he was first arrested. She had been thinking of herself, and her future.

"You're coming with me. I believe you, but I need to get shit resolved. I need both of them to be dead, and gone."

She gripped the counter, recalling the way *he* laughed at her screams. The way he looked so damn smug when she had woken in the hospital to find out what they'd done. Jeff Wright, the one man she wanted to kill more than anything else in her life. She truly believed she could kill him without care or thought.

"What happens to me after?" she asked.

"I don't know. That's up to you, and if you get cold feet, we'll handle it."

"You'll kill me?" She was finding it hard to not be scared. This Gash scared her and he was nothing like the man she once knew. This man could easily kill her without a second thought.

"We'll have to wait and see."

Charlotte stared at him for several seconds. It may have even been minutes as she looked at the man who had haunted her dreams for years. She'd once been in love with Gash, wanting him from afar. For one night, she'd gotten her dream, only to have it shattered the next morning. It was part of the reason she'd taken the damn promotion, to get away from him and from Rebecca. Her heart had been fragile, and witnessing Gash with Rebecca had broken a part of her over the days they had been together. Whenever she thought of her feelings about Gash, she was always all over the place. There was no set feeling. She loved and hated him. He made her sad, angry, and aroused. He was bad for her.

"I'm tired." She had enough drama for one night. The best solution was for her to just sleep, and end this uneasiness inside her. Everything looked better in the morning.

Without waiting for him to give her instruction, she left the kitchen, and walked the few steps toward her room. Her apartment was modest, and her only bathroom was through her bedroom. She closed her bedroom door, which had no lock. Charlotte had learned long ago to not even bother putting a lock on her bedroom door. If people wanted to get into her apartment, they could get inside without any struggle, and she would be sent to her fate.

Taking a quick shower, she didn't take her time, enjoying the peace and quiet. Gash had invaded her apartment, and ruined any kind of peace she thought to have. Her night shirt was hanging on the back of the door, and once she finished with her shower, she dried quickly, placing the towel over the radiator, and then getting dressed.

She walked back into her bedroom, and came to a stop when she saw Gash already in her bed.

"What the hell are you doing here?" she asked. He could have taken the floor in the sitting room, or the small couch. She didn't want him in her room, not now, not ever. It brought back too many memories, and tonight she was really struggling to keep all of those memories locked up tight.

"Getting comfy." He snuggled into her bed, which pissed her off.

"Get out."

"No."

"This is my bed, and you're not going to take my bed from me."

"I'm not taking it from you, babe. Far from it." He patted the bed. "Join me."

"No, get out." She moved toward her dresser and started to brush her hair. "This is my room. You're the one attacking me, coming into my apartment, and you weren't even invited. Get out." She placed her brush back down on the dresser, and stared at him. "Well?"

"I'm not moving," he said. "You may as well get in."

Gritting her teeth, she folded her arms, and glared some more. "Why are you being a pain in the ass?"

"Because it's awesome to be so."

"Whatever. You're not going to move?"

"Nope, and I'm going to stay right here, and this bed is damn comfy." He wriggled a little, sighing as he did.

Asshole.

****

Gash wasn't going to move, but he liked it when Charlotte did. Her tits, without the bra constraining them, bounced, and her nipples were rock hard pebbles, pressing against the front of her shirt. He wanted to see her without that shirt, to feel her body next to his, and to fill his hands with her full, rounded tits.

Desire hit him hard, and his cock thickened. Moving on the bed, he did his best to hide the evidence of his arousal so he didn't frighten her. Charlotte always seemed like a little mouse to him, ready to scurry away. At least that hadn't changed about her.

"Fine! I'm not going to give up my bed." She stomped to her side of the bed, and withdrew the cover. Charlotte pushed it back enough for her to see his naked thighs. "You're naked. What the hell are you doing in my bed naked?"

"I don't wear clothes to bed." He hadn't worn clothes to bed since getting out of prison. For five years he was forced to wear the colors of the prison he was in. He'd made a vow that he would never, ever wear shit like that again. "Don't worry, babe, I won't bite."

"Put some clothes on."

"No. It's not going to happen."

She released that growl again and climbed into bed. Gash watched as she gave him her back, then moved, thumping her pillow.

"You know, some people believe that the whole tossing and turning could be down to sexual frustration."

"Shut up."

"I could relieve you if you want me to." He wanted to. Damn, he wanted to touch, to taste, and to fuck her so bad.

"Gash, you may be stronger than me, and be here intent on revenge on two people I despise, but if you lay a finger on me, I will kill you."

He laughed. Her threat was so cute, and he told her so.

Again, another growl, and more thumping. He loved hearing that little growl. It made his cock harder than fucking rock.

Gash rolled over and stared at her back. Her wet hair trailed down her back, and he reached out to stroke her hair.

"Do you have a death wish?"

"I'm touching the hair on *my* pillow. I'm not invading your space."

She was so tense, and Gash settled down on the pillow, suddenly interested in what she'd been doing with her life. "What has happened to you the past seven years?" he asked.

"Why?"

"I'm curious. You know I was in prison, and then I was with the club. What have you been doing?"

"Nothing. Living life."

"And there's no boyfriend?"

"None," she said.

"How long has it been since you were with someone?" he asked.

"None of your business. Gash, we're not friends."

"We're not enemies."

"Yes, we are. I don't make a habit of being nice

to men who grab me around the throat as a way of a hello."

He may have been a little drastic with his introduction.

Seven years he'd waited to see her again.

Not once had she tried to see him, not even to visit him in prison. Gash had always waited to see if she would turn up. They hadn't been total BFFs, but he'd always thought they had some kind of connection.

Watching her back, he waited as she grew soft, and slowly gave into sleep. When she was completely asleep, he thought about the couples at the clubhouse. Lash and Angel were a force to be reckoned with. The love between them was strong, and Gash had witnessed what true love really was. He'd always thought it was a fantasy, but being released from prison, he'd seen his Skull brothers falling, or having fallen in love. The club was still tough, and the men were not the kind to be messed with. Gash had felt out of place. He was filled with anger and a need to kill. The brothers, they needed him to be the better man, to be the man he'd been before he'd been incarcerated. That man was dead.

Sliding across the bed, he moved his hand beneath her head, and molded against her back. He gripped her hip, and breathed in her scent.

Home.

This felt like heaven to him, pure heaven, and for a change, he didn't feel like leaving this moment.

Closing his eyes, he allowed himself to finally relax, and fall into sleep.

****

Lash stared up at the clubhouse, wondering what he was going to do. Devil had been in touch, and Master had threatened the Chaos Bleeds women. His first instinct was to open his home, and to allow the man to send them to The Skulls. He liked Devil, and it had upset him when the two clubs had fought, separating. They had survived many enemies by working together. Tiny had screwed that up with fear, and it was the one time in Gash's life where he didn't agree with his then-Prez.

The club, it was busier than ever. They had some of their nomad men staying with them, Adam, Twisted, and Happy. Fighter, Baker, and Ink were now full-fledged members. That had been one of the biggest decisions he ever made for the club. Initiating three new members, he had to be sure that they were loyal to the club, and wouldn't put anyone else before them.

"Son, you should be in the club, cuddled up against your wife," Tiny said.

"This coming from the man who has a new baby at home."

"Something told me you needed to talk." Tiny shoved his hands into his pockets and sighed. "It's cold out."

"Yeah, it is."

"You're doing good, Lash."

"If my father was here, I wouldn't be doing this right now."

"Lash, your father and mother died for this club. I took you and Nash in because it was a bad decision on my part that got them killed. They loved the club." Tiny chuckled. "Your mother, she was a firecracker. She loved the club, but she also wanted your father to know that you boys were going to have a choice. They would fight, but I swear it only made them both mad for each other. It's why your mother called you Nigel and your brother Edward."

Lash remembered his parents, or at least small memories of happiness. He didn't like being called Nigel. Even Angel didn't call him that. He fucking hated the name. What kind of biker was named … Nigel? He recalled his parents, the few things that he'd not forgotten. His mother loved baking, and his father loved building shit. God, it seemed like a lifetime ago since he thought about them.

"Being a leader was always going to happen, Lash. It's not just about being a hard ass or having muscle that makes a good Prez, a good leader." Tiny rocked back on his heels. "I've been a good and bad one. I learned on the job. After shit went down with The Darkness, I knew I wanted Fort Wills to be a town that everyone felt safe in."

"Devil wants me to create a safe house for their women."

"A war is coming, and we have to be ready. I fucked up with Devil, but this is your call on what you make."

"What would you decide?" Lash asked.

"Son, I'm not about to give you the answers you're looking for. I didn't have anyone to rely on when I had to make a choice. It's not easy, and I know it fucking sucks, but you've got to have faith in yourself. What is your heart telling you?"

"My heart?"

"It's corny and shit, but your heart is in the club. Your woman, Angel, I never would have put her as a strong woman, and she's certainly proven that I can be wrong. She's strong enough to take on the club women, and she doesn't even need to use violence."

Lash smiled, thinking about the last few months of him training her, not only to fight but to also use a weapon. She was becoming one hell of a shot. He was never going to piss her off or risk getting his dick blown off.

"What do you want to do?" Tiny asked.

Taking a deep breath, he stared up at the clubhouse. It had been broken into, burnt down, rebuilt, and invaded. This was his home, it was his life, and he was never going to leave it.

"We're going to have Devil's back when his enemy comes to call. Chaos Bleeds, they're our allies, and it's time the world knows it."

Tiny nodded, slapping his back. "Go and rest. There's plenty of time to fight, but resting, it's a luxury during times of war."

They made their way into the clubhouse together, and Lash didn't wait around. He headed toward his room, and opened Anthony's door first. His little boy was sleeping. Anthony was already in school, and learning fast. Resting his head against the doorframe, Lash watched him sleep before entering his room.

Angel was curled up on her side, looking beautiful like always. He removed his clothes quietly so he didn't wake her.

As he climbed in behind her, she released a sigh. "Where did you go?" she asked.

"I had some thinking to do."

"Did you come to a decision?"

"Yes, I did. We're going to help Devil."

"I knew you'd come to the right decision." She wriggled into his arms, and he cupped her stomach.

"You know I was going to let the Chaos women come here?"

"It's the right thing to do. It's why I love you, and I'll always love you no matter what you do. You're a good man."

He would never understand Angel, but he loved her with his whole heart.

Chapter Three

Charlotte was so warm, and it felt so good to be warm. She opened her eyes, and frowned as she blinked sleep from her eyes. It had been over seven years since she had a good night's sleep free of nightmares. She became aware of a rock hard body at her back with a thigh between hers.

That was something she'd never woken up to. Gash had been completely out of it the night they had slept together, and there hadn't been any kind of snuggling like this.

Glancing behind her back, she saw that Gash was wrapped around her. His large body held her in place, not letting her move.

"Stop moving," he said.

"You're awake."

"It's hard to sleep, babe, with you moving around all crazy. Just go back to sleep."

"You're holding me!" She yelled the words, shocked that he was holding her. It had been the best night's sleep of her life, and now she knew why. Gash had been wrapped around her, and she couldn't think of any other excuse as to why she slept so well.

"I've not slept like that in years, and it feels so damn good."

She tried to wriggle again and came into contact with his dick. He was rock hard. Charlotte didn't know what she was expecting, but it wasn't that.

"Is that what I think it is?"

"Moving on my dick is not exactly going to help the situation, babe. You're turning me on, and I love a nice warm pussy in the morning."

"I'm not yours."

"You possess a nice pussy though. I bet if you let loose one time, you'd be soaking wet and begging for my cock."

"Shut up."

"Nah, I don't want to shut up." The hand on her stomach moved down, and before she could stop him, he cupped her pussy between her thighs. "That's it, baby. Don't fight what you want, and give yourself a chance to have what you want."

"I don't want you."

"You don't? How long has it been since a man has touched this body, Charlotte?" His hand slid beneath her night shirt and touched her intimately.

Charlotte couldn't fight the arousal that rushed around her body.

"I feel how wet you are, babe. You're soaking wet, and I'm not even touching the lips of your pussy. Open up for me, and I'll show you what a good time is really all about." As he was talking, he'd already slid his hand inside her panties and started fingering her pussy. "Ah, there she is. You're so wet, Charlotte. You're coating my fingers." He kept teasing her pussy, and Charlotte, she couldn't fight anymore. It had been over seven years since she was with a man, and she couldn't hold back any longer. Spreading her thighs, she moaned, and he pressed two fingers inside her as his thumb stroked over her clit. "That's it, Charlotte, let go, and give me those cries."

Moaning, she closed her eyes, and thrust her pelvis up against him.

"Fuck, baby, you're so hot. How did I not know this? I'd have taken you out for a test drive."

It was like a bucket of cold water was thrown over her.

They *had* been together, and it had resulted in

something that had sent her crazy. Slamming her elbow against his stomach, she jumped out of bed. Gash cursed, releasing her long enough so that she could get free.

"Don't touch me." She was shaken to the core, and her body was on fire for his touch. Two completely different emotions, and it was sending her already sensitive mind haywire. This was not the way to handle the situation with Gash. He was back in her life for them both to kill Rebecca and Jeff. Then it would be finished between them with either him killing her, or them parting ways. She didn't see any future between them. The moment his hands were on her, it had reminded her of how they had once been together, and that wasn't going to happen again. Gash would destroy her, and he didn't even have a clue of the kind of power he had over her. Only *she* remembered what happened between them.

"I'm sorry. You were hot for—"

"Don't. Don't be an asshole. Are we leaving today?" she asked. The sooner she got this done, the happier she'd be.

"Yes. If we make good time."

"I'll get ready." She had no intention of lingering with him.

She grabbed some clothes from her wardrobe, and rushed into the bathroom. Sitting on the toilet, she rested her elbows on her knees, and took several deep breaths.

Everything is okay.
Just breathe.
You're alive.
You're alive.

She chanted over and over in her head as tears filled her eyes.

You don't need him.
You're stronger than anyone.

In that moment, she didn't feel strong. She was weak. One night he'd been back in her life, and she'd been ready to let him play with her. Charlotte couldn't even blame him. She'd known he was drunk, but it didn't stop it from hurting any less. It wasn't going to happen. There was no way she was sleeping with him. She was stronger than that, and she wouldn't give in to him.

"Charlotte," Gash said.

"Go away. I'm getting dressed."

She wiped away the tears that she hadn't realized had fallen. Standing up, she stared at her reflection, and was transported to a distant memory.

"It's done," Jeff said.

"Done?" Charlotte croaked out the word, holding the blanket up to her chin. "What's done?"

"You don't really think we'd let you carry his child, did you? It's so stupid what you did, Charlotte. You were never supposed to be part of this, but I guess you just couldn't help but stick your fucking nose in where it doesn't belong." Jeff pressed his hand against her head, and leaned in close. "Now, you will pay."

"You took my baby?" she asked.

"You were going to fight us, Charlotte."

She whimpered, and placed her hands on her stomach as she was overcome with a deep wave of sadness. "You killed it?"

"Yes. The baby you had, it's now gone."

Charlotte screamed. Reaching across to the pitcher of water, she slammed it against him. The pitcher smashed, and as she grabbed a shard of glass in her hand, not caring that it cut her deeply, she tried to attack him. Her body was not her own, and as she stood on the glass, pain shot between her thighs, and on her feet. She tried to attack him, slashing him with the makeshift blade.

Charlotte came out of the memory, and shivered. Nurses had rushed into the room, strapping her down. The next time she came to, Jeff had been gone, along with her baby, and she had tried to kill herself. After trying to end her life three times, she was committed to a psychiatric hospital where she spent the next five years trying to ease the pain in her heart by using every chance she had to take her own life. It was only when a good doctor finally got through that she started to fight. It was ironic. Gash got out of prison at the same time that she got out of a hospital. She wasn't the same woman who entered that hospital, and for the past two years she had tried to make a life for herself.

Gash coming back into her life had given her the best kind of medicine that he didn't even realize he was offering. He gave her a chance at revenge, at killing the man and woman who did this to her.

Staring at her reflection, she wiped away the last of her tears.

You can do this.

She pictured Jeff Wright in her mind, and how damn smug he thought he was. Coming back from her business trip to discover that Gash had been falsely accused of rape and murder, she'd been about to get in touch to tell them the truth about Gash. Charlotte had heard the date that Gash was supposed to have raped Rebecca then murdered her boyfriend. She knew without a shadow of a doubt that it wasn't him because that night, Gash was with her, making love, giving her a baby that was later torn from her. Gash would have known she'd be able to help him because when he woke up the next morning, he'd seen her.

Charlotte had been his alibi, and he'd known it, which was why he came after her. He didn't know what they did, what they made together, nor what was taken from her. Gash had known he'd been at the apartment that night with her, and that was all.

Getting dressed, Charlotte tied her hair back and made her way out to the kitchen. Gash was at her stove cooking pancakes, or better yet, he was burning them.

"What are you doing?"

"Cooking breakfast."

"We can eat on the road." She grabbed her purse and jacket.

"I'm sorry about this morning in your bed," he said.

"You're apologizing?"

"I've never taken something that wasn't offered before in my life. I'm ashamed of myself, and even though we were once friends, and now I consider you—I don't know what I consider you—it's still wrong."

His apology took her by surprise.

"Okay, wow, I accept."

"Good." He dumped the pan into the sink, and moved toward her. She couldn't look away as he pulled his Skulls leather cut onto his shoulders, and ran fingers through his hair. He really was a good looking man, and one that always affected her.

Think about Jeff.

She and Gash were never going to have a relationship. Too much crap had passed for that to ever work.

****

It took several hours to get to Fort Wills, and they made a couple of stops for eating, and toilet breaks. Gash loved having Charlotte on the back of his bike. He made her wear a helmet, and she clenched him tightly as they rode. Part of him was tempted to make the trip last longer just to have her wrapped around him a bit more, but he didn't do it. Pulling into The Skulls clubhouse, he saw several brothers repairing their bikes, and a couple of the club whores having a smoke.

Pulling up next to Steven, he waited for Charlotte to climb off his bike, and when she was about to fall into a heap, Steven kept her upright.

"It's all right, baby," Steven said.

Climbing off his bike, he was about to move Steven out of the way when the brother took Charlotte's helmet off for her. In the process, her hair was pulled out, and Gash couldn't look away as she ran fingers through it. The brown of her hair, and the strands fanning out, triggered a memory. He remembered that hair sliding down his body before she took his cock into her mouth.

Shaking away the dream, he took hold of her hand, locking their fingers together. Again, he didn't know why he needed to hold her, only that he had to.

"So, who are you?" Steven asked.

"I'm Charlotte."

"Well, Charlotte, I'm Steven, and I'm the guy you need if you want me to rock your world."

"Her world is already rocking. Back off," Gash said.

"You got dibs."

"She's mine."

"Whatever, man, it's your call. I'll go back to my bike. Weather says it's about to snow or some shit, and I don't want my baby in trouble."

Rolling his eyes, Gash made his way toward the clubhouse.

"He seemed nice."

"He's not."

"I'm not your girl."

"You're not a club whore, Charlotte. Until further notice, you're mine."

They entered the clubhouse, and he wasn't

surprised to see kids running around the clubhouse. There was a time when this place was for men only. Now, it was just a family clubhouse, or at least, during the day it was. He spotted Blaine and Emily in the corner, talking. Their daughter would be in school along with Miles, Tabitha, Rachel, Anthony, and Sally. Sally was Whizz and Lacey's adoptive daughter who was fifteen years old.

Angel came out of the kitchen with Markus walking behind her. Markus was Kelsey and Killer's son.

"You're back," she said, the moment she spotted him.

She gave him a big hug, and he released Charlotte long enough to hug her back. Angel was exactly as her name suggested, an Angel. There was a time when he first got out of prison when he believed Angel was trying to break her wedding vows and fuck him. He'd been wrong, dead wrong. She wanted to be his friend, and that was all. Her love for Lash was strong, and she would never cheat.

"Angel, I'd like to introduce you to Charlotte."

"Hey, Charlotte, it's lovely to meet you," Angel said, drawing the woman at his side into a hug. Angel just couldn't help it. She saw the good in everyone, and at times it worried him that she was going to end up dead for it.

"Angel? Is that like a club name or something?" Charlotte asked.

Gash glared at her, but Angel laughed it off.

"You would think so, right? Nah, it's my real name, and I'm not joking around."

Charlotte was red. "I'm so sorry. I don't really know much about the whole MC thing."

"And yet you're friends with Gash."

"I wouldn't call us friends."

Angel smiled. "You're the first person that I know who he's invited here. That would make you his friend."

"You're back already?" Lash asked, coming up behind Angel. He held her hip and reached out to shake his hand.

"Yeah. Lash, this is Charlotte. Charlotte, this is our new Prez, Lash."

"Nice to meet you."

"You're the one he's been looking for? The one who helped put him in jail."

Charlotte tensed. "No. I'm not."

"Leave it, Lash. She had nothing to do with it."

"And you believe her."

"Yeah, I do. Charlotte has never had a reason to lie to me, and I believe that."

Lash glared at her for a few seconds, and Angel patted his chest. "I believe it as well."

Once Angel talked, Lash listened. It was kind of a miracle to witness actually. Gash wished he'd been at the club to see the two fall for each other. The way the others talked about it, it had been something awesome to watch. Instead, he only watched them together.

"Did you hear the good news?" Lash asked.

"Good news?"

"I'm pregnant," Angel said, placing her hand over her stomach. "I finally convinced him Anthony needed a play friend."

"Anthony's at school now," Gash said.

"I know, but I'd like to think he wants a little brother or sister." The smile dropped from Angel's face. "What if he doesn't want a brother or sister? What if he hates us?"

Lash shook his head, cupping her cheek. "No. I'll talk with Anthony, and he'll love us having a big family.

Why wouldn't he? He's always around Tabitha, Miles, and the others."

Angel sighed. "You're right. We're expanding our family."

"Do you know where Whizz is?" Gash asked.

He could be around Angel all day. She helped to ease the bitterness inside him, and make him forget his need for revenge. He didn't want to ever forget what he planned for the two people who put him in prison. It was his mission to end them, and he was going to do it while laughing.

"Whizz is at home. Since they adopted Sally, they spend a little more time at their own place. Lacey doesn't want to force the MC onto Sally, and to give the girl a somewhat normal life," Angel said.

"Sally's at school."

"Whizz has set up this nerd station in one of his rooms at his place. Several screens, internet, and all that shit that makes him a certified nerd."

Gash chuckled. A lot of people wouldn't believe that Whizz was not only a computer geek, but he was also one tough asshole. He had a lot of respect for Whizz, especially as the man had survived some of the worst kind of torture that he had ever heard about.

"Then I guess we're paying Whizz a visit." He grabbed Charlotte's hand and headed out of the club.

As he was leaving Killer was walking into the club.

They shook hands and slapped each other on the back.

"Wasn't expecting to see you so soon," Killer said.

"What can I say? You just can't get rid of me."

"Tell me about it. Can't stay, about to head out." Gash made the introductions with Killer and Charlotte.

"Where's Kelsey?"

"She's at work." Kelsey worked as a dental nurse, and had returned to work not long ago. "I'm here to pick up Markus."

"Angel has him inside."

"Great."

They said their goodbyes and headed back toward his bike.

"I have to say I'm shocked," Charlotte said.

"About what?"

"Your MC life. I thought it was drugs, booze, and sex."

Gash laughed. "Well, it's got the sex and the booze. It's also about being a family. The Skulls, they're my real brothers and family."

"What happened to your real brother?" she asked.

"My brother?"

"Yesterday, you mentioned a brother."

Gash released a sigh. "I'll talk to you about that another time. I've not seen him in years, well over a decade. He's probably dead."

"And you don't care about that?"

"My brother was an asshole, Charlotte. Believe me, he's better off dead, otherwise he'd have hurt every single person he could get his hands on."

Charlotte frowned. "How do you know that?"

Gash sighed. "Can I just promise that I'll tell you soon? I want to get to Whizz."

She nodded. "Sure. You're not obligated to share anything with me." She placed the helmet on her head, and he swung his leg over the bike. Charlotte climbed on behind him and held him tightly.

Gash liked the way she held onto him.

Starting up his bike, he rode out of the clubhouse, all the time aware of her pussy pressing against his back.

When he got out of prison, he'd fucked every single club whore, and then he'd gone around them again, wearing out all the women. He loved sex, but with Charlotte, it was something more.

Thinking back to this morning when he had his fingers inside her pussy, he'd been desperate for her to find pleasure. Usually he didn't give a fuck about whether the women got off or not. With Charlotte, it meant more.

Get over it.

She's not the one for you.

You're using her to find peace.

Her legs tightened around him, and he gritted his teeth. There wasn't going to be anything between them other than two people looking for revenge. He could do this, and place Charlotte in a little box for him to deal with.

Chapter Four

A woman with red and blue hair answered the door, and Charlotte loved the colors. It looked amazing on her as it wasn't glaringly bad, or anything. She fingered her ponytail as she'd pulled her hair back, and her brown locks were dull and boring.

"Gash, what are you doing here?" she asked.

"Hey, Lacey, I'm here to see Whizz."

Lacey turned and yelled Whizz's name. "Come on in."

"What are you doing now?" Gash asked.

"I'm actually in college right now. I'm taking beauty courses, and putting my love of dying my hair to good use."

"Beauty?"

"Yep. I'm loyal to The Skulls, and the old ladies are more than happy to let me work on their hair." Lacey smiled, looking at Charlotte. "I could do wonders for your hair. It's so long."

"You're not touching her hair," Gash said.

Tugging out her ponytail, Charlotte stuck her tongue out at Gash. "What do you recommend?"

Lacey chuckled. "I like you."

"I'll probably be dead before you can do anything."

She noticed that made Lacey pause.

"Excuse me?" Lacey asked.

"Gash is threatening my life. I don't know how much time I've got left."

Gash slumped. "I'm not going to kill you."

Charlotte looked at Gash and shrugged. "You're the one that has been threatening to kill me. I accept my fate, and if I don't make it out alive, then I don't."

"This is weird," Whizz said. "Talking about your death should have you at least a little freaked. Normal women would be freaked out, even Lacey, and she's not that close to normal."

"Hey!" Lacey said, chuckling at the same time. They were a strange couple, but seeing them both together, it worked.

Charlotte smiled. "I've had a lot of time to deal with it."

"You're Charlotte," Whizz said, moving toward her.

Lacey didn't stop running fingers through her hair. "Purple, it would totally rock purple, and a trim. I bet we could put some curls in the length, and it would totally look fuckable."

Gash groaned.

"I tell you what," Charlotte said. "When we finish what we're doing, you can do whatever the hell you want with my hair."

"Deal." Lacey glared at Gash. "She better be back in one piece, or I'm going to start making some serious use of the knives that Whizz gave me for Christmas."

"Lacey, keep Gash company. I want to talk to Charlotte."

Before she could protest, Whizz was dragging her down a long corridor into a large room that looked like a command center.

"Wow," she said. "That's a lot of computers."

"Yes, it is. This is my office. Welcome." Whizz closed the door, and Charlotte leaned against the wall that had nothing against it, no technology, and nothing worth breaking.

"I don't want to touch anything in case I, erm, I break it."

"Have you told him?" he asked.

"Told him?"

"About what you lost?"

Charlotte tensed up. "No one knows about that."

"There's always a trail, Charlotte. No one is clear from shit like a forced abortion. There had to be paperwork."

She pressed a hand against her stomach as tears filled her eyes.

"The suicide attempts, along with every other shitty thing that you've been through." Whizz kept his distance, and she was more than happy about that.

"I ... I didn't think anyone would know what happened."

"Gash asked me to find information on Rebecca and Jeff. You came up, and I gave him the way to locate you."

"Wait? You told him?" Why hadn't Gash asked? Why did he assume she helped put him in prison?

"No. I didn't give him everything." He moved away from his position opposite her toward his wall of screens. "To be honest, the information for me, it only gave me more questions. You see, abortions, documents, all of that stuff I can follow, but I cannot follow emotion. I don't know what happened between you and Gash, or between Jeff and Rebecca. Only the paper trails, and possible security footage. It's a lot in this day and age, but it's not everything."

She listened and watched as he clicked on the keyboard, and her life came up on the multitude of different screens.

Whizz moved away, and she forced herself to face the life that she had been trying to forget.

Pictures of herself before and after her life was turned upside down. Hospital images of her injuries and files of her diagnosis were displayed for her to see.

"I didn't give him this. Gash doesn't know that when you tried to testify on his behalf, you were drugged and shipped to a hospital to have the baby that you had created together, torn out of you."

Her heart was racing. This was her secret. This was what Jeff did to her, and what Rebecca did to her. They held her down, forced her to sleep, and removed something so precious to her that she had already been making plans for her future. The promotion had come first, and then when she landed, she'd gotten the positive test, and for those few precious minutes her life had been perfect. A few minutes, that was all she got.

"Gash didn't know, and he still doesn't know," she said.

"He still doesn't know. You're the woman from his dream. The woman he had sex with, and can't remember it."

She nodded.

"I was away when Gash was arrested. I got a promotion, and that was why I was out of the country. When I got back, I discovered he was on trial and I was going to testify on his behalf. I'd been feeling sick, and the only explanation I had was being pregnant. I took a kit, but Jeff was there, and Rebecca." Her cheeks heated. "Before him, I was a virgin, and I've never been with anyone else. Sad really, I know."

"That's not sad. Everything that comes with you returning, that's sad, that's unbearable," Whizz said.

"Everything had gone to shit in the time that I was away. Gash was being done for murder and rape. I knew he was capable of murder, but not out of jealousy. Gash didn't give a shit about Rebecca, or who she screwed."

"How did you know?" Whizz asked.

"He came around one night when she was

entertaining another man." Charlotte laughed. "I was so embarrassed that I couldn't even talk. Anyway, Rebecca was always really loud. He came and laughed. Said Rebecca was an easy girl, and he'd wait his turn. No jealousy. He even picked up a cooking magazine, and read it while Rebecca was screwing another guy. Then, when the two came out, Gash shook the man's hand, and grabbed Rebecca."

"Wow, I didn't know that."

"Not everything is written on a computer, just like you said," Charlotte said. "He's not a rapist. Gash would never hurt a woman."

"Yet he hurt you."

She cupped her neck and shook her head. "I guess I'm not considered a woman in his eyes."

"And yet for a short time, you were the mother of his kid."

Charlotte flinched. "That's a long time ago."

"He or she would have been seven years old, entering his eighth birthday."

Tears filled her eyes, and before she could hold them back, they fell down her face. "Please, stop." She started to shake as the pain took over her entire body. For a little over two years she hadn't experienced this. Two years, at least she'd known a struggled peace.

"Gash doesn't know what he lost."

"He wouldn't believe me." She wiped the tears away.

"You need to tell him."

"You knew all of this, so why didn't you tell him?"

"Some things are best said by the person who suffered through it."

Charlotte snorted. "He tried to kill me."

"Did he *really* try to kill you?"

"He had his hand wrapped around my neck, about to choke me."

Whizz sighed. "I didn't know him before prison, but something tells me if Gash intended to kill you, you'd be dead. He doesn't leave people alive if he can help it. He's a hard ass."

"So, I should be grateful he didn't want to kill me?"

"No, you should think about the fact he hasn't."

Charlotte licked her lips, staring back at the screen. "Why didn't you tell him this?"

"I believe people deserve second chances. My wife, Lacey, she was going to kill me—well, she couldn't kill me. It's complicated. Anyway, I don't believe you and Gash got your chance. Now it's time for you to get your shot together."

"He doesn't want me."

She stared down at her large figure and sighed. When she was trapped in a mental ward, she'd actually slimmed down to a size eight. She couldn't eat, and the doctors ended up forcing her to eat. The moment she got out of the hospital and started making her way in the world, she promised herself she'd stayed slim. Then her pain would only be eased by baking and cooking in the kitchen. Her size eight didn't last long. She had remained a size sixteen for the past two years, and she no longer believed in diets. Her life had already sucked enough without taking out her love for food.

"You'd be surprised what a man wants."

"We're looking for Rebecca and Jeff."

"I get it. Okay, let's go and invite Gash back into the room before my wife tries to kill him."

"Lacey? She'd kill him."

"Lacey's an interesting character. I love her, but Gash, he doesn't like her smart mouth."

She smiled.

Following him out of the nerd room, she saw Gash was glaring across the counter in the kitchen as Lacey sang out of tune at the top of her voice.

"Getting her out of the clubhouse hasn't been good for her," Gash said.

"What? I love her singing." Whizz walked toward Lacey, kissed her on the mouth, and smiled at his wife.

Charlotte's chest hurt. She had never experienced that kind of love.

Her own life was all about work and sleep.

Life truly sucked.

****

"We want to find Rebecca and Jeff," Gash said. He'd had enough of hanging around Lacey. Just being around the weird woman irritated him. After everything that had happened to her, she was too damn happy. Charlotte wiped her cheeks again, and he noticed her eyes were red. What the fuck had Whizz said to her?

"How do you expect me to do that?" Whizz asked. "If I could find her, I would."

"Tell him, Charlotte."

She rolled her eyes. "Have you seen that room he has set up? I'm surprised he hasn't found her already. You said so yourself, there's always a paper trail."

"Yeah, there is, but some people can make shit disappear, and it takes a little longer to find it. Tell me what you've got, and I can go ahead and find it." Whizz took a muffin that was on the counter, and bit into it.

Charlotte frowned as she watched him turn green then spit out the chewed up muffin. "Babe, you used salt in place of sugar."

"What?"

Lacey took the muffin from him and bit into it, doing exactly the same thing that he had done. "Shit, I sent Sally to school with two of them."

"Yeah, she's going to throw them in the trash."

Whizz filled a glass with water and then nodded toward his room. "Let's go."

Gash waited for Charlotte to follow, and she did so with her arms folded. He loved her attitude, the fight inside her. She wasn't broken.

Entering the room, Gash was amazed. "Shit, I thought your room at the clubhouse was damn creepy."

"Now I can control my own world." Whizz did a maniacal laugh, then sat down. "So, what did I miss?"

"I don't know if you missed it or if it didn't go anywhere. In the city there was this apartment she went to that was supposed to be in her name."

"Give me a second. When I did a search under her name, no apartment appeared. It would have if she bought it or even rented it." Whizz started clicking, and the speed with which his fingers were moving were giving Gash a headache. The bastard wasn't even staring at the keyboard but at the screen.

"Nope, nothing is registered under her name. Only her residence, which is your old address, Charlie."

"Charlie?" Gash asked.

"What about it?" Whizz said. "I figure she and I are going to be good friends."

"I don't mind," Charlotte said.

"Lacey's a bad influence."

"I say that every time she rides my dick."

Gash glared, and Charlotte laughed. "Is this the whole MC image thing?"

"You bet. Now, back to crime fighting. There's nothing here. Rebecca was a poor girl, with a shitty job, and no hope out of her shitty life. Do you have an address?"

"She wouldn't remember," Gash said, pissed that

it was another fucking dead end.

"Actually, I do."

"How did you remember that?" Gash asked. "It has been over seven years."

"She put the address on the refrigerator, and it's what I saw for months, and I recited the shit out of it while waiting for the kettle to boil," Charlotte said. "She was always bragging about how she bagged this rich guy." She shrugged, holding her hand out. "There's not a lot to say. Rebecca was easy."

"She sounds like a fucking whore," Whizz said.

Charlotte gave Whizz the address, to which his club brother whistled.

"What?" Gash asked.

"It's a fucking good part of the city. I'm talking seriously elite, exclusive kind of shit." Whizz shook his head. "Rebecca may have found herself a sugar daddy, or she was in deep shit."

"Deep shit?" Charlotte asked.

"You get into that kind of apartment three ways. You're either rich—Rebecca wasn't. You're fucking someone who is rich, or you're a criminal with money, and I'm talking high shit in the criminal world, mafia kind of money."

Gash shook his head. "That shit's not good."

"No, it's not." Whizz kept on typing, and something red came up.

Gash saw access was being denied, and Whizz simply kept on whistling while typing away.

"What's he doing?" Charlotte asked in a whisper.

"Nerd shit."

She smelled so good, and Gash fisted his hands to stop himself from reaching out to her. What was it about Charlotte that made him want to touch? To caress? To fuck?

Shit, she was driving him crazy with the need to fuck her.

He wasn't some damn stupid adolescent boy who'd never known a fucking cunt.

Running a hand down his face, he held in a groan as his cock thickened when Whizz whistled.

"Well, fuck me," Whizz said.

Looking up at the screen, Gash frowned. "What is that?"

"It's the owner of the apartment. It wasn't in Rebecca's name, but whoever that man is, he wanted it kept secret."

Gash stared at the photograph of the man, and something seemed oddly familiar about him, but again, he couldn't figure out what.

"Who is it?" he asked, then looked toward Charlotte. "Do you recognize him?"

"Not a clue."

Whizz did some clicking. "This used to be Rebecca's apartment. It's registered to Rebecca and Jeff, and there is the signature of the deed. The date here is just before the supposed murder and rape, so they didn't own this for long before you were arrested, Gash."

Charlotte moved in closer to the screen. "Enhance his face."

Whizz zoomed in and clarified the picture. "That's Jeff."

"That's not Jeff."

"I'm telling you that is Jeff." She pointed at his eyes. "I won't ever forget those eyes. Do you have an old image of Jeff?"

Whizz nodded, clicking away once again. He did some kind of scan, and there it was, a perfect match. "There are some things people can't handle, and having your eyes changed, clearly was one of his."

"Do a complete background check on him," Gash said.

"Well this man is not Jeff anymore." Whizz started pulling up bits of data. "Look, this is going to take me some time to get everything—"

"Just give me a name, and an address. I can do everything else," Gash said.

"And go in with half the information, and get shot the shit out of?" Whizz asked.

"Four years I've waited."

Whizz slammed his keyboard down and stormed up to Gash. "You spent five years in fucking prison. Boo fucking hoo, you had three square meals a day, and out of the five fucking years, I bet you didn't have to fight every single one of those days. I was trapped, caged up, and fucking tortured for hours. I was taken, Gash. I know that pain. If you think I'm making you wait on purpose, then find someone else. I don't know you from way back then. I know you now, as my club brother, and a man I'd die for. Give me the night to get every fucking thing you need so you don't get yourself and Charlie killed."

"I'm going to leave you two alone." Charlotte left the room, closing the door behind her.

The moment the door closed, Whizz wrapped his fingers around Gash's neck, and threw him up against the wall. "I was repeatedly raped. My ass ripped open, and I was helpless to fight. Don't let me make a mistake, and let you walk into the same kind of hell. This is what I do, but it takes fucking time." There was a darkness, a pain, and a helplessness inside his eyes that made Gash relent.

"Fine."

"You and Charlotte can stay the night. I'll work through the night to make sure you're ready to leave."

"You don't have to do that."

"I want to do that."

Gash gripped the back of Whizz's neck and pressed his forehead to his. "I'm sorry."

"She's in love with you, Gash."

Releasing his friend, Gash shook his head. "She can't stand me."

"There's more to Charlotte than she lets you see. Give her a chance, and she'll surprise you." Whizz turned away and started working on his computer.

Leaving the room, Gash was kicked in the balls. He cupped his dick and stared at Lacey.

"Don't ever put him in that place again. Whizz cares about the whole of the club. His loyalty will get him killed one day. He puts his life at risk every time he digs deep into places he's not supposed to go."

"You didn't have to kick me in the balls."

"I did. You only know one language, and that language is violence. I will protect my man. Charlotte is in the kitchen. I've hired her to cook for me. You've got a better chance of leaving without food poisoning."

Lacey stepped over him and entered the nerd room.

Fucking bitch packed a punch. Getting to his feet, he made his way back into the kitchen. Charlotte was chopping up some vegetables and gave him a small smile.

"She got you on kitchen duty."

"Told me unless I want takeout, I've got to cook."

"Angel's tried teaching her how to cook, but it seems the only thing she knows how to do is her hair." Gash shook his head. Charlotte didn't say anything, and kept on chopping. This was what he remembered about her from the past. She didn't speak unless she really needed to. He'd always tried to make her talk, to bring her out of her shell. "You didn't scream in there?"

"Did you get out what you needed to?"

"Yeah."

"Then I'm fine with that. You're the kind of guy who needs to shoot first and ask questions later. That's up to you."

"You think that's different?" he asked.

"It's different to how you used to be." She shrugged. "I wasn't the one that went to prison—"

"Where did you go?"

"What?" she asked.

"When I was sentenced, where were you?"

Tears filled her eyes, and she stopped chopping. "I'm not ready to tell you."

"You've got something to tell me then?"

"Yes. I've got something to tell you."

"Will it make me angry?" he asked.

She took in a deep breath. "I don't know if you'll be angry or if you'll even care. I'm not ready."

Gash nodded. "I'll stop asking until you're ready."

****

Stink watched Sandy cleaning the dishes, and sighed as he leaned against the doorframe. She was always running away from him, and he really wished he knew what to say to her to make her understand he didn't give a shit what she once was.

"You're staring."

"I like staring," he said.

"It's creepy."

He chuckled. She placed the final plate on the draining board, and dried her hands on a towel.

"You're getting the whole stalker image down."

Stink shrugged. "I've been told to keep your ass safe."

"It was over a year ago, Stink. I'm fine, and you don't have to keep me safe."

"The club rules, Sandy."

She sighed again. "I'm thinking of going back to my own place."

He tensed up. Sandy was a doctor, and she had been part of the club who'd had it rough several times. She had stopped screwing the single brothers years ago, but there was a time she'd screwed everyone. He'd never taken a taste of what she had to offer even though he always wanted to. Instead, he kept his distance, watching from afar to make sure no one claimed what he'd known from day one was going to be his.

"You're leaving the club?" Stink asked.

She moved toward him, standing right in front of him, and he got the scent of cinnamon that always seemed to cling to her. Sandy was the most beautiful woman he'd ever seen. She was in her late thirties, and a doctor. He knew without a doubt that she could do so much better than him.

"I think it's time that I moved on." She touched his cheek. "I'm not an old lady, and I'm no longer a club whore. I'm nothing."

Cupping her cheek, he pressed his head against hers. "You're everything, baby."

She chuckled. "You could have fucked me years ago without any kind of commitment, yet you didn't even give me a chance."

"I knew from the moment I first saw you, you'd be different."

"Stink, you deserve better."

He took hold of her hands, staring down at their hands, touching, together. "I don't give a fuck who you've been with before. I know what I want, and I know I can make you happy. The past couple of years, you've been happy. I've made you happy."

"There hasn't been any sex between us."

Stink pressed her up against the nearest wall, trapping her hands in his. "Do you really think it wouldn't be epic between us?" He held both of her hands within one of his, and started to caress the tips of his fingers down her arm, across her breast, and down to cup her pussy. "I can show you how fucking epic it can be between us. If you think for a second that you know anything about me and what I'm capable of, think again."

"The club is not my home."

"We're your family, and I'm your guy. I'm not going to let you go without a fight. You belong to me." Slamming his lips down, he claimed hers, letting her know without a shadow of a doubt that he was the master of her.

Chapter Five

"This smells good," Lacey said.

Charlotte turned to see a young girl following behind Lacey. She offered them both a smile, unsure what to say.

"Oh, shit, Charlotte, this is my daughter, Sally. Sally, this is Gash's friend, Charlotte."

"You cook?" Sally asked.

"Yeah, it was a condition of staying the night." Charlotte frowned, looking between the two.

"Cool, we don't have to worry about takeout. Dad doesn't like to hurt her feelings, but Mom can't cook. I'm going to go and do homework." Sally kissed Lacey's cheek, and headed out of the kitchen.

Lacey looked ready to cry.

"Are you okay?"

"Yeah, I'm fine." She waved her hand in front of her face. "I, erm, I can't have kids, and being able to adopt Sally, and now she's calling me mom—it's a dream come true."

"Did you adopt her at a young age?" Charlotte asked. Her own heart was breaking over the child she had lost.

"No. It was only a few months ago to be honest. Sally fought us both at the beginning. Whizz told me she was acting out in case we sent her back to her foster home." Lacey took a seat.

"You wouldn't do that?"

"I know it's strange, adopting a kid that will probably be going off to college, but I saw Sally, I saw how broken she was, and I just knew I could help her. Whizz and I, together, we could help her. We're not perfect ourselves, but we make a good life."

"You make a good team."

"I like to think so."

"Will you adopt more?"

Lacey sighed again. "I hope so. We've spoken to Sally about it, and she doesn't mind. We're looking into adopting once everything settles down at the club."

"I hope Gash and I are not a problem—" Before she could finish saying anything more, Lacey held her hand up.

"No, you're not a problem. You'll come to learn in the MC life, it's always hectic and chaotic, but there are moments where it's peaceful. You'll learn to embrace those peaceful moments, and be happy about it. You and Gash are more than welcome here. I just wish I could have made you something delicious to enjoy. I'm not exactly good in the kitchen."

Gash chose that moment to enter the kitchen. He stretched out his muscles, and Charlotte couldn't help but stare at his hardness. His muscles were so big and thick, and she felt like a complete girl just looking at him.

You're a woman.

He was much bigger now than he was seven years ago, and back then he'd been ripped.

Charlotte, stop it. You're not seriously thinking about a guy being ripped?

"Showing off, are we?" Lacey asked.

Gash lowered his arms, which she found disappointing.

"We know you've got the muscles and the hot body. There's no need to brag." Lacey rolled her eyes and jumped out of her chair. "I'm going to go and check on Whizz and Sally. Don't fight, kids."

Charlotte chuckled. "I like her." She spoke once Lacey had left the kitchen.

"She's interesting."

"You don't sound like you believe that."

He laughed. "What can I say? She's a little eccentric for me. Whizz loves her, and yeah, that bastard didn't really smile for a time when I got out."

Charlotte had seen the scars on Whizz's face, and even the ones on his hands. She knew all about scars. The last thing she would do was stare at someone with visible marks on their body. She had her own scars, and not all of them were on the outside of her body. There were some on her wrists and on her body where she'd gotten desperate. Her scars were deep within her heart, and she hoped that helping Gash would ease the pain that was always there, making it hard for her to breathe at times.

Staring at the chicken stew, she looked at the red sauce, which reminded her once more of blood. Pushing the thoughts to the back of her mind, she moved to the pantry and found some dried pasta to cook.

"What put that sadness in your eyes, Charlotte?" Gash stood behind her. She hadn't even heard him move. His hands gripped her hips, and she closed her eyes. Charlotte loved his touch, always had, and it had been her downfall.

"I told you I'm not ready."

"Did Jeff hurt you?"

Opening her eyes, she turned off the tap, and moved out of Gash's arms to put the pot on to boil.

She went to tuck some hair behind her ears but paused when she realized her hair was up in a ponytail.

"Did he?" Gash asked.

Staring at him, she nodded. "Don't ask me how he hurt me, but he did."

"Okay, why did he hurt you?"

Licking her lips, she took a deep breath. "When I came back home, you had already been arrested, and the evidence had been building against you. The moment I heard what was happening, I tried to put a stop to it. I wanted to help you. I know you're not a rapist. I know you're capable of murder but not a jealous murder. Jeff and Rebecca were there at the apartment, and let's just say they made sure you were already sentenced, and I wasn't in a good enough state of mind to help you."

"There are a lot of holes in that story."

"I'm not ready to tell you those holes. Maybe one day I will be." He was going to find out the truth. Jeff would laugh in his face, and it would blow up. Charlotte's heart started to race, and everything fell away. Why was she hiding her secret? What did she have to gain from it? Gash would forever be doubting her, and the only way for him to realize she was on his side, was by giving it to him straight. "Actually, you know what? I'm tired of hiding this. Remember you asked if there was a woman who used to visit our apartment?"

He nodded.

"You remember fucking a woman, right? You were drunk? That woman was me, Gash. Yeah, that's right. You fucked me. We had sex together, and the next morning, you didn't even remember it. I figured I'd just forget about it, too. I got this big promotion at work and was asked to go to England for a business meeting, and while I was away, that was when you were arrested. When I finally got home, I suspected I might be pregnant because I'd been off my food and everything. I took a test, and I found out I was pregnant." She saw she was shocking him, and it was tearing her apart talking to him. But this had to be said. If she didn't, Jeff would spill the truth, and the last thing she wanted was for that fucker to ever think he had any more power over her. "You didn't use any protection during the time we were together. We were pregnant, and I was going to tell you once I helped testify on your behalf. I wanted you to be involved, and I knew it was going to be a challenge to make you realize that we had slept together. Jeff and Rebecca were there. They saw the test that I had taken, and they knew I was going to the cops to give my testimony. I was stupid, and I told them I knew you were innocent. To cut an even longer story short, the night you were accused of committing the murder, you were with me. I remember the day because it was the best day of my life. I knew without a doubt you couldn't have done it. Rebecca was framing you."

"What happened to the baby?" Gash asked. "I know what fucking happened to me. What happened to our baby?"

Tears filled her eyes as she stared at him.

"Jeff drugged me up as I was about to leave the apartment, and he had Rebecca's help. The next thing I knew, I woke up, and he had my baby aborted. After that, I went a little crazy, and let's just say I've been trying to kill myself every chance I got."

Gash stepped forward, taking hold of her hand, and turning it up. She stared at his bent head, refusing to look at the scars that covered the inside of her wrist. She saw them every single day, a constant reminder to her. When she was at work, she covered them up with long sleeves. There were times she forgot that they were there. With Gash staring at them now, she relived the relief that she felt when she pressed the broken glass into her skin. She'd tried to end her life with broken glass, metal, anything that could cut into her skin.

Each time, before death would claim her, she'd been saved.

Her doctor on the last time had stayed with her, talking, and asked her to consider the fact that maybe she was still alive to give someone a message.

"We had a baby?"

"Everything you need to know is with Whizz. Excuse me." Charlotte couldn't stay with him after revealing her soul to him.

Leaving the kitchen, she made her way outside and took several deep breaths. The garden was small, but it had a chair toward the back. Taking a seat, she stared up at the cool sky.

"Are you okay?" Sally asked.

Charlotte turned, surprised to see the young girl sitting on the patio, doing her homework.

"I thought you were inside?"

"I like working outside. It clears my head." Sally shrugged. She had a blanket wrapped around her. "Are you okay?"

"I'm fine." Charlotte stared up at the stormy sky. "It's going to start raining soon."

"There's snow forecast," Sally said.

"Figures."

Sally didn't say anything else, and Charlotte couldn't help but look back at the young girl. "Are you happy?"

"I am. The Skulls, it's a family, and with Lacey and Whizz adopting me, I've finally found a place for myself. Besides, I'm always protected."

"Protected?"

"The guys and the prospects, they all work to protect us. Some of the brothers pick me up, and bring me home. I like it. For once in my life, I'm actually safe."

Sally went bright red, and Charlotte just knew that she had a crush on someone. It had been too long since she had been young, and falling in love. There were times she wished she could still be like that.

****

"I need the folder you have on Charlotte." Gash leaned against the door. His entire world was turning upside down, and right at that moment, he couldn't focus for shit. The woman he'd spent years dreaming about was none other than Charlotte, the woman he'd always liked but always overlooked. The woman he believed he could never have.

"You know?"

"She just fucking told me. It's not true, man. Tell me it's not true." Gash didn't want it to be true. He didn't want her to have gone through that kind of shit on her own. Fuck, he'd been so consumed by himself that he'd not even thought about anyone else.

Whizz didn't say anything. "I've just finished printing her stuff out."

"Is it bad?"

"It's worse, and you'll get everything you need in there. There's a spare bedroom upstairs on the right. It's where I'm going to put you and Charlotte tonight."

Gash thanked him and walked upstairs. His hands were shaking, and when he closed the door to the bedroom, he sat down on the bed and stared at the folder. He saw the sheets of paper peeking out at the edges, taunting him.

Closing his eyes, he finally saw Charlotte, the woman without a face, and she fit perfectly. He'd fucked her hard, and taken what he wanted without asking. Charlotte had submitted to him, giving him everything he wanted, and they had been perfect for each other.

Opening the file, he started to read, Charlotte's words ringing around his head. Twenty-four hours ago, he'd been intent on hurting her, and yet because of her association with him, she'd been the one hurt.

She wanted to help him, and on the paperwork in front of him there were calls, proof that she had tried to reach out to him. Gritting his teeth, he read through every single piece of paper, even down to Charlotte's admission.

He even chuckled, though he felt anything but laughing. Charlotte had been pregnant with their kid, and then she'd had it torn from her. She had gone to a mental facility at the same time he'd been sent to prison, and released the exact same day that he had.

Fucking shit!

Throwing the file to the floor, he started to pace the bedroom. This was all just too damn much for him.

"Fuck! Fuck! Fuck!"

He'd always assumed that he'd been the one fucked over. Now he learned that not only had Jeff and Rebecca fucked him, they had also fucked over an innocent. Charlotte had been an innocent. She shouldn't have been brought into this shit, and yet she was.

Even now he remembered her as a shining light, always smiling and laughing with him. Just being around her had made him feel good. He'd always tried to make her laugh, which wasn't hard to do.

Since he'd seen her again, Charlotte hadn't laughed or joked. The carefree woman was gone, and in her place was a broken one. Anger filled him, consuming him, and there was nothing he could do to give her back what had been taken from them.

Moving toward the window he paused. Charlotte was still outside, and she was staring up at the sky. Did she even realize the way she was sitting? Her legs were out, and her hands with her palms facing up. It was the same position that she had taken in one of the pictures as she'd been interviewed. There was no life inside her.

"You've both been broken," Whizz said, startling him.

"What the fuck are you doing here?"

"I thought I'd come to see how you were getting on. Lacey's ruining what Charlotte did of dinner."

"You knew this when I asked you to do the search?"

"Yes."

"It's why you didn't want me to go hunting for her?"

"Charlotte has suffered enough. She doesn't need to be used by you to find out more truth."

Gash gritted his teeth to stop himself from crying. He just wanted to scream and cry, and hurt someone. Jeff Wright. He was going to hurt that son of a bitch, and when he was done, he was going to make sure that the bastard wished for death long before he even got it.

"They tortured her," Gash said.

"She was helpless."

"I know." He'd not been there to help or save her. Instead he'd been locked in a cell, and spent his days planning to hurt those who had put him there. "I didn't help her."

"Dude, you couldn't help her. Don't beat yourself up about shit you couldn't control. You can help her now, and that is all that counts."

Charlotte's face was turned up to the sky. There was no smile on her face, and she was staring up at nothing. Her face was blank.

"When I was threatening her life she offered to kill Rebecca providing I kill Jeff."

"I'm not shocked by that." Whizz shrugged. "What are you going to do?"

"She was carrying my baby."

"I think you need to touch on the fact that not only was she carrying your baby, you didn't even remember putting it inside her."

"Everything is totally fucked up."

"Do you care that you screwed her?"

Gash glared at him. "What kind of fucking question is that?"

"I'm just trying to make sense of it, man."

"Sense? You want sense? How about this? For the past seven years I've been curious about a fucking woman that I didn't think existed. Only it turns out that not only does that woman exist, but she's been someone I've been harboring hatred for because she didn't come and help me. When everything I've been thinking is fucking lies. Charlotte needed me. She was pregnant with my kid, and I fucking failed her." His voice had risen to the point of yelling. He was so angry. This time he was angry at himself, and how stupid he had been.

She had been there, and tried to save you.

She went to hell along with you, and you'd not even known it.

The first thing he did when he saw her again was choke her. *Fuck, crap, shit.* He hated himself.

"I had a kid."

"Did you remember her?" Whizz asked.

"I remembered bits of the night, holding her, feeling her wrapped around me. It's what got me through the worst part of prison. I need to go talk to her." Gash wasn't going to run away. All he wanted to do was forget about the shit that she'd been through, focus on his own pain, but that wasn't the kind of man he was. Years ago, it's what he would have done, but now, he wouldn't even dream of doing it.

Now was not the time to shirk his responsibilities.

"We're here if you need us," Whizz said. "I'm going to keep on looking, and you can stay here until you need it."

Gash nodded. In moments like this, he appreciated the club. The Skulls gave him the family that he never had. They were his brothers, which was why he never sought out his own brother. He didn't even know what had happened to Andrew. They had both come to the club together, and Andrew had failed to make the grade when it came to The Skulls' standard.

Pushing thoughts of his brother out of his mind, he made his way outside. Gash paused when he saw Sally on the ground, studying.

Sally looked at him, then toward Charlotte. "Okay, I'll look scarce."

He waited until Sally was gone, and the door had closed giving them some privacy, or as much privacy as they could have in the garden.

Charlotte was nibbling her lip, and he moved toward her.

"That was fast," she said.

"I read the file. I didn't need to read all of it." He'd glanced through some of the pages. Gash knew as much as he needed to about the situation.

"Do you still think I know where Rebecca and Jeff are?" Charlotte chuckled.

"Don't do that. Don't make jokes." He knelt down, holding onto her knees.

Tears were once again in Charlotte's eyes. "You were drunk. I never expected you to remember what happened. You thought I'd put you to bed after passing out."

"I don't remember the day clearly."

"You were my first," she said.

Gash winced. "You were a virgin."

"Yep. How unlucky am I? Not only do I have sex for the first time with a man so drunk he doesn't know his own name, but I get pregnant the first time." Charlotte shook her head. "I guess I asked for what I got."

He cupped her cheeks, forcing her to look at him. "No, you didn't get what you deserved." Unable to hold back any more, he took possession of her lips. It was a simple kiss, and yet it was totally right. Pulling away, he wiped the tears that fell down her cheeks, hating the fact she was crying. "We made a baby?"

"Yes."

"I'm going to kill Jeff. I will make him suffer, and make him wish that he never looked in your direction."

"Do you forgive me?" she asked, sobbing.

"You've got nothing to forgive, baby. Nothing at all. I'm the one who should be asking you for forgiveness."

"Why? There's nothing to forgive you either, Gash. I know you didn't want to have sex with me. I shouldn't have let it get that far."

She was staring down at her hands, which lay in her lap.

Gash didn't know what to say. Charlotte had always been unreachable to him. She was the kind of woman a man like him couldn't have. He wasn't a good man. He had killed people and didn't care that he'd ended lives. When he first met Charlotte, she had always been the sunlight. She reminded him of purity, love, and everything he'd sold his soul to never have.

"You deserved better than a man like me. I'm not a good guy. I'm a fucking evil bastard, Charlotte."

"Stop it."

"No. You're an amazing woman. I loved spending time with you, but I knew I wasn't the guy for you. You're the kind of girl who deserved someone who was gentle, kind."

"You don't know me at all," she said. "I was attracted to you, and you gave me the most amazing night of my life. When I woke in the morning, reality came back, and that sucked."

"And you got pregnant. Were you going to tell me?"

"I told you that I was going to tell you, Gash. I knew I had to make you believe that we'd been together. You deserved a chance to be a father."

He took a deep breath to stop himself from falling apart. "I'd have believed you."

"You don't know that."

"I know you. That fucker took away our chance to be together. We would have been happy, Charlotte. I'd have made you my old lady, and no one would have ever hurt you."

"Seven years, Gash. We would have had a seven year old child."

Pressing his head against hers, he gripped the back of her neck, holding her tightly.

"I will end him, Charlotte."

"Not without me. You're not leaving me behind. I need this, Gash."

They would have to do this together, and Gash wasn't going to let her go.

Chapter Six

"I can't believe this," Angel said, coming out of the kitchen of the club. Anthony trailed behind her. Eva looked up from the table where Miles and Tabitha were doing their homework.

"What is it?"

"I've just got a call from the school. Daisy's parents have left her there. I picked Anthony up, and I had thought about taking Daisy home, but the teacher wouldn't let me. Now, they can't get in touch with her parents, and the school decided to contact me." Angel growled. "They really annoy you."

Eva laughed. "You can swear if you want. The kids hear enough around their dads."

"I'm not interested in adding to their vocabulary. Will you watch Anthony while I go and get her?"

"I want to go," Anthony said.

"I'll go, too. She's my best friend," Tabitha said. "Her mommy's mean to her."

Angel's heart sank. She had done her best to keep Lash and the boys out of it. This was not the first time that Daisy had been left at school, waiting to be picked up. If she didn't pick her up, Eva would, or one of the other women. Daisy was best friends with Tabitha, and they'd been close since the two had started nursery. Angel wanted to take Daisy away from her drug addict parents, but so far, their lawyer had advised not to get involved. She didn't like to cause conflict, and even though Tiny had given the parents a talking to, she didn't want more trouble.

"I'll be back soon," Angel said.

"Take one of the prospects with you."

In that moment Twisted, one of the nomad men

who was taking a chance of settling down in Fort Wills, entered the kitchen. "I heard you needed a prospect? I'm better than a prospect." He gave a bow.

"I've got to go and pick up Daisy, and take her home." Angel sighed. "Are you sure you're okay with that?"

"Yes. I'll drive."

She took hold of Anthony and Tabitha's hands, and walked them toward the car. Once they were seated, she climbed into the passenger seat, and waited for Twisted to take them toward the school.

"Daisy's parents are bad news," Twisted said.

"You know them?"

"I've heard of them. Bad people. Addicts always are." Twisted didn't take his eyes off the road.

"I don't want to leave her there."

"We don't have a choice. The guys can give them warnings, but unless the state does anything, we're stuck."

Angel hated this. She hated feeling helpless.

When she pulled up outside of the school, Daisy stood with the principal, Mr. Dean Mint.

Climbing out of the car, she smiled at him. "I'm sorry."

"Angel, you do not need to apologize. I've notified social services of this."

Daisy was staring at her feet. Angel's heart went out to her. "It can't go on."

"I don't know if it will do any good. I will do what I need to do to keep her safe." Dean looked tired. He was a good principal and tried to keep the kids safe.

"You do the best you can." She reached out. "Come on, Daisy. Tabitha is waiting for you."

She gave Dean a final smile, and led Daisy away to her car. There was already a spare car seat in the center of the back seats.

"Mommy forgot about me again," Daisy said.

Cupping her cheek, Angel sighed. "I know, honey. I didn't forget about you."

"Will you be my mommy?"

Angel would in a heartbeat. "I can't now, baby. We'll see what happens." Securing her in her seat, she blew out a breath and climbed back in the front.

"It would solve a lot of problems. I bet her parents wouldn't even know she was missing if you took her home now."

Glancing behind her, she saw Tabitha and Daisy were talking. Checking on Anthony, she saw her son held onto Daisy's hand, and was staring at her.

"Take me to her trailer park," Angel said.

She wouldn't allow Daisy to go without, not on her watch.

"She likes you," Twisted said.

"Are you trying to convince me to adopt her?"

"Why not? You can adopt her, or Lacey could. She'd be happy to have a kid."

Angel blew out a breath, rubbing at her temple. This had to stop.

They pulled up outside of Daisy's parents' trailer park, and she heard the shouting all the way in the car.

"I'll be right back," Angel said. There was a time she'd have run in the opposite direction from any kind of confrontation. For Daisy, for the club, she'd learned to stand tall, and to fight for what she believed in. Lash and even Gash had given her more confidence. The Skulls had helped to enhance her life.

Knocking on the door of the trailer, she waited. After a minute, she knocked again.

Nothing.

She raised her hand to knock once more, but the

door flung open, and she had no choice but to step back.

"What the fuck do you want?" Daisy's father asked.

Angel couldn't recall his name, and the fumes coming from him made her feel sick. She placed a hand to her stomach, remembering she was carrying another child, and she needed to be careful. "You forgot to collect Daisy from school."

"What the fuck are you talking about?"

"Your daughter? Daisy?" She turned toward the car and watched as Twisted climbed out of the car.

The concern for her unborn child made her more relaxed to see that Twisted was there. She couldn't help but smile. If Lash was here all hell would have broken loose. Her husband wasn't exactly known for liking addicts. After everything that went down with his brother Nash, who got addicted to drugs, Lash couldn't stand them. They were no longer allowed within the walls of the club, nor did the club have anything to do with them.

"What the fuck that little bitch done now?"

****

"Daddy looks angry," Daisy said.

"Angel will fix it." Tabitha squeezed her hand.

Daisy loved being around The Skulls. Her parents, they didn't care about her. They always forgot about her. If they forgot about her at school, they also forgot to feed her. Her parents were not like those of The Skulls. Daisy had learned that at a young age her parents were not like others. Not every parent drank bad stuff in the morning, or sniffed white stuff up their noses. She loved being able to sleep at Eva's or the clubhouse with the rest of her friends.

"Your mom is nice," Daisy said, turning toward Anthony. Once again, he was staring at her. He was a strange boy, always staring, observing.

"You'll be safe now. Mom won't let anything happen." He squeezed her hand a little tighter.

She rested her head against his shoulder. It would be nice to be safe. Her parents were always shouting and screaming, and hurting each other. For once, she'd just like to know what it was like to be wanted, to have a mommy who hugged her, kissed her goodnight, and read her a bedtime story.

Her father started to shout, and Twisted moved away from the car.

Closing her eyes, Anthony wrapped his arms around her, and Tabitha hugged her back. She didn't have much, but she had friends.

****

Late that night Angel paced up and down the length of her bedroom. They were not at the clubhouse, and Daisy was sleeping with Anthony in his room as the spare room didn't have a bed yet. Lash sat on the edge of the bed, staring at her.

"You want us to adopt her?"

"Yes. This is not the first time they've left her, Lash. They don't deserve their daughter. They were drunk, and I couldn't leave her there."

After bringing her home, Angel had done homework with Anthony and Daisy, made dinner while waiting for Lash to come home.

"Look, babe, I know you want to adopt her, and I don't want to see her go back to those fuckers, but you're carrying, and Anthony, he can be a handful." He got to his feet, pulling her into his arms, and stopping her from pacing. "You can't hide the fact that you're struggling with this pregnancy. You're sick, tired, and exhausted. If I'd known that Daisy was still at school before you, I'd have gone to get her myself."

The pregnancy was exhausting her, and she'd

even noticed that she was sleeping a lot more, and the simplest thing made her tired.

"I can't send her back. Don't make me."

"Lacey and Whizz," Lash said.

"Huh?"

"They adopted Sally. Lacey loves kids, and I recall seeing her around Daisy. She'd happily have her as a daughter."

Tears filled Angel's eyes. "Don't you want a daughter either?"

"Angel, babe, I love you, and I'd love to have Daisy as my daughter. I'd take care of her, and Anthony would be her brother, but I told you before, you're my main concern. It kills me to give Daisy to Lacey when I know you'd love her like your own. But you can't handle another child right now, and I'm going to be taking care of you. You come first."

"I could handle it."

"Daisy will be loved, and she won't go far."

"What about her parents?" Angel asked, crying. Her emotions were all over the place. She couldn't stop crying, and she hated it. Even as she was crying, she was hating herself, wondering why the hell she was crying.

"I'll pay a visit to the family, and they won't have a problem. I'll get our lawyer to do the paperwork, and we'll go there together."

Resting her head against Lash's wide chest, she let out a sigh. "I love you."

"I love you, too."

Chapter Seven

"How did you burn pasta?" Charlotte asked, staring at the burnt strands of linguine.

Lacey sighed. "I put the pasta into the water, and I forgot about it. I went to sit with Whizz."

Charlotte stared at the other woman's face, seeing that she was blushing. "I see."

"What?"

"You were doing more than sitting around." Staring into the pot, she saw the water had boiled away, and the pasta was just wrong. "You might want to throw the pot out."

"That will be your fifth pot this week," Sally said.

"I'm trying, okay? I can't cook." Lacey took the pot out of the kitchen, and Charlotte stared at the stew.

"Do you have bread?" Charlotte asked.

"Yes. Dad makes sure we have bread in case Mom ruins dinner, or won't let us call for takeout." Sally moved to the far side of the kitchen, and opened a large cupboard. "Tada."

Chuckling, Charlotte gave the stew a final stir. "It's ready."

"I'll go and get everyone."

Carrying the large pot into the dining room, she placed it on the center mat and made her way back into the kitchen. Gash was entering the kitchen, and wrinkling his nose. "What could she have possibly burned now?" he asked.

"Pasta. I didn't think it was possible, but it is." Charlotte didn't know how Lacey had lived her life with the way she burnt things.

She grabbed several bags of buns and paused in the kitchen. Gash was still there, and now that he knew the truth, she didn't know what to say to him. Opening her mouth, she closed it once again. What was there to say?

Heading back toward the dining room, Gash stopped her. He held onto her arm. "Were you going to live the rest of your life waiting for me to come to you?"

Glancing over her shoulder, she shook her head. "I was just trying to get on with my life. I didn't know if Jeff was going to come back for me, or if I'd done my time. They kept me alive, which has always been a question for me. I'd have been better off dead." She shrugged. "I didn't exactly plan anything in my life. I've just dealt with everything that has come my way. I'm still alive, so I always figured something else was going to happen."

She loved his touch.

The pleasure from the brush of his fingers was making it hard for her to focus. "What about you?"

"I was going to kill you because I truly believed you were part of it. Now, I should take you back home and let you live in peace."

"Peace? You think going home now will help me find peace? I need this, Gash. I need to put an end to this." She would beg if she had to. "What happened between us is over, I get that—"

"Is it?"

"What?" She frowned, confused.

"Over, between us."

She paused. What the hell was she supposed to say? After everything that had happened to her, she'd never once blamed Gash. Sure, she'd been pissed at him for not remembering their time together, but she had taken advantage of him, so she shouldn't expect anything, and everything with Jeff had been on him, not on Gash. She'd always blamed Jeff, and that fucking bitch Rebecca. From the moment she saw her, Charlotte should have listened to her gut, and kept her away from her. She had ignored her gut feeling, and allowed Rebecca inside.

"I don't know what you want me to say?"

He cupped her cheek and pressed her against the doorframe. His large body surrounded her, stopping her from moving. Staring into his dark eyes, she couldn't help but bite her own lip. There were times she still fantasized about what those lips felt like on her body. It had been so long since she'd felt him. Seven long years of remembering.

"You kept me sane. My memory of you, and our time together. I may not have remembered it was you, Char, but I knew I was with someone, and I wanted that feeling again."

"I'm not some toy for you to play with."

"I know. I'm not hoping to take you out to play with you every now and then. I've found you again, and I don't want to lose that. I don't want to lose you."

This was not what she had expected. "There's a lot of history—"

"We can't change the history that is between us, but we can rewrite our future. Don't shut me out. Give me a chance to prove to you that I wouldn't have just walked away from you. That night seven years ago, Char, you took a part of me with you, and I've never had it back."

Gash shocked her even further as he took a kiss. It was a tender kiss, his lips pressing against hers.

"I'll take these into the dining room."

He brushed past her, and Charlotte grabbed onto either side of the wall of the door frame. Her pussy was soaking wet like it always was with Gash. Her body craved his touch like her lungs craved air. This was a fight that she could never win no matter how much she tried.

"Wow, that looked kind of hot," Lacey said.

Opening her eyes, she found Lacey in the doorway, arms folded and smiling.

"You heard?"

"Yep, I think you guys should give it a chance. You both were torn apart from one another, and that just completely sucks." Lacey sighed. "We're all in the dining room."

Nodding, she followed Lacey to the main rom. Whizz, Gash, and Sally were already there, waiting for them. Taking a seat, she accepted the bowl that Whizz handed her. The chicken stew looked tasty, and her stomach growled.

She sat beside Sally, who was handing out the bread rolls.

"It has been a long time since we had a good, home cooked meal."

"Angel did the last one. She sent home some soups and lasagna," Sally said.

"Okay, okay, I get it, all right? I'm trying, and Angel is even trying to teach me how to cook. Nothing is working." Lacey glared at each of them.

"I can cook," Sally said. "How about I give it a try for the next week, see what you think?"

Whizz tilted his head to the side. "You can cook?"

"Yeah," Sally said.

"I'm game if you are," Whizz said, turning to Lacey.

"We're supposed to be looking after her." Lacey sighed.

"I can't stand anymore takeout food, and we can't expect other women at the club to cook for us."

Charlotte glanced across the table to see Gash laughing. "You were totally unlucky in picking one of the few women at the club that can't cook."

"I wasn't originally part of The Skulls," Lacey said, glaring at him.

Smiling, Charlotte dipped her bread into the sauce and listened to the couple debate with each other about how they were going to keep on eating for the remainder of their lives. It was funny to watch. Whizz and Lacey were very much in love, and Charlotte saw the bond between them. Sally was giggling as well, and the atmosphere around the table was one of friendship and love.

"This is really good," Sally said.

"I'm pleased. It would taste great with pasta as well."

Lacey sighed. "It's good with bread."

"Did you burn the pasta on purpose?" Charlotte asked, trying to repress laughter.

"Totally. I love my bread, my carbs."

"She's totally lying," Whizz said. "She can only handle some coffee in the morning, and pouring cereal into a bowl."

"You do realize that you will pay for this," Lacey said, looking at Whizz. "I can find other ways of making sure you're not a happy man." Lacey raised a brow.

"Ew, gross, you took it to the gutter," Sally said. "I have young, delicate ears." She covered her ears and had a disgusted look on her face.

"Do you see what I have to put up with?" Gash asked.

Smiling, Charlotte enjoyed the feeling of having a family. It had been so long since she'd felt this happy, and being around Gash and his club helped. In that moment, she no longer felt sad or in need of taking out revenge on the bastard who had ruined her life. At least Gash knew the truth.

The reality of their situation crashed through, and Charlotte lost her appetite. Leaving the bread in the bowl, she listened to the conversation around the table without saying anything. At the end when she made to take the dishes, Whizz stopped her. "You cooked, we'll clean up."

"You go and freshen up," Lacey said. "I left some clothes out for you. They should fit, or they might be a little bigger."

Nodding, Charlotte made her way toward the bedroom. Lacey had already told her where she'd be sleeping that night. Opening the door, she made her way toward the bed, and sat down. Sinking her fingers into her hair, she closed her eyes, taking deep breaths.

You can do this.

You can do this.

Squeezing her eyes closed, she concentrated on her breathing, and was instantly taken back to a memory.

"You said it would get easier." Charlotte sobbed the words out as best she could. It had been two weeks since she had last tried to take her own life, and the pain hadn't gone away. Doctor Williams had promised her that she would start to feel better.

"Charlotte, I promised it would get easier, but I said it wouldn't happen right away. It's going to take time."

She gripped her head, screaming as loud as she could. "I've got to go. I've got to help him. He doesn't know, and he's in prison."

Doctor Williams touched her knees, and she couldn't help it. She lashed out, hitting him hard. Charlotte attacked him, needing to get out. She only landed a few blows before he took over, pinning her to the chair. The door to his office opened, and she saw the nurses waiting to inject her with something to make her relax. She didn't want to relax. Charlotte wanted them to miss, to kill her, or let her take the needle and finally end her life.

"Stay back," Williams said, shouting at his employees.

"Sir—"

"This is what she wants, isn't it, Charlotte? You want us to react so we give you an opening that means you can take your own life?"

He held her tightly so that she couldn't move. Williams was damn strong for a doctor, and she had underestimated him. Tears spilled from her eyes.

"Let me go!"

"No. I'm not going to let you destroy yourself."

Gritting her teeth, she watched as the nurses left his office, and all fight left her. She was exhausted, tired, and fed up. "I'm tired of fighting. I'm tired of feeling," she said.

"How we react to circumstances within our life is what defines us, Charlotte."

"That's a nice way of saying that I'm fucking up."

Williams sighed. "You're in pain. You've been handed a life that you don't deserve. I'm going to make sure I can help repair the damage that has been caused to you."

"You can't fix me. I'm not some kind of puzzle."

"I know, but I can create a foundation within you that makes you strong enough to fight. I can't let you out of here, Charlotte."

"What do I have to do?" she asked.

"You've got to learn to fight the pain, to keep on trying."

Gash entered the room, pulling her out of her thoughts.

****

"What's wrong?" Gash asked.

Charlotte had disappeared from the table, and he'd seen the change within her. As he stared at her now, the smiling woman was gone, replaced by this sorrowful shell. She looked like Charlotte, acted like her, but it wasn't her. Seeing her like this, all he wanted to do was find Jeff and Rebecca. Before heading upstairs, Whizz had promised to have the information he needed by the end of the night.

"Nothing."

"Don't lie."

"You have a wonderful family."

"Charlotte?"

She shook her head. "It's okay, really. I'm fine. I'm just thinking that once we handle Jeff and Rebecca, that I need to make sure I still have a job when I get back."

"You really think I'm going to let you go back to your real life after all of this?" He closed the bedroom door, not wanting anyone to hear their conversation. Charlotte was a private person. Gash wasn't that insensitive, and he remembered everything about Charlotte. The night they shared together was still foggy in his mind, but he was so damn happy knowing it was Charlotte. He'd been attracted to her even back then, but she reminded him a little of Angel. She was the kind of woman a man like him looked at but didn't touch.

"Once you get what you want, there's going to be no need for me here."

"Seven years ago I fucked a woman and I thought I was hallucinating. Seven years ago I was accused of rape and murder, and sentenced to a prison cell. Seven years ago, you were put through hell because you tried to help me. You may think there's nothing between us, but I'm not going to deny shit between us."

"Gash—"

"No, I'm not going to make excuses. We would have had a chance if I had fucking remembered that we were together. This is real between us, and I'm not going to be the one denying it. You belong to me just like I belong to you."

Tears filled her eyes, and he sank his fingers into her hair, turning her face to stare at him. "We've got a history, and it's time we had a future together. Too much has been taken from us. Don't let them win, Charlotte."

She smiled. "You sound like my doctor."

"Doctor?"

"Doctor Williams. I was his patient for five years, and he's the one that supported me when I finally got sane enough to leave. He saved my life several times, and became my rock. He still checks in every now and again to make sure I'm still strong."

He didn't like the sudden strike of jealousy that hit him. Gash didn't even know the doctor, and yet he didn't like the relationship he'd started with Charlotte.

"I'm here now." No one was going to take care of Charlotte but him.

"I'm not ill, Gash. I'm fine, and I'm sane." She chuckled. "Apart from the fact I've agreed to kill someone with you. That's a bit fucked up."

He laughed along with her, and that felt good. "Where have I been without you?" he asked.

"I don't expect anything from you."

Pressing his head against hers, Gash took a deep breath. "Expect shit from me, Charlotte."

"You were going to kill me twenty-four hours ago."

Unable to take it anymore, he slammed his lips down on hers. It was like she awakened the fire inside him. Gash would fight everyone to be with her. She was never getting away from him. He'd nearly lost her once, and that shit wasn't going to happen again. They had lost each other, and they had lost a child together. Fuck, they had lost a child together.

It broke him just thinking about it, and Charlotte had gone through that all on her own. He'd been in prison, too caught up in his own problems to give a thought to what was happening to Charlotte. His woman had needed him, and he'd failed her. Not only that, he'd thought the worst. Pressing her back against the bed, he didn't release her lips. Instead he deepened the kiss, plunging his tongue inside her open lips. Releasing her hair, he captured her hands and placed them above her head. Linking them together, he held her hands in one of his while he explored her body with his other. She was so fucking full and ripe. Her tits were huge. The pictures of her with all of her weight gone fucking scared him. Charlotte was a full figured woman, and he wouldn't have her any other way. He would make sure that he took care of her.

No one would ever hurt her. They would have to go through him first, and he was a fucking brick wall.

Prison had taught him not only to fight, but also to fight through the pain.

Charlotte wrapped her legs around his hips, and he pressed his dick against her jean clad pussy. They were both clothed, but that didn't matter in those moments. Gash was drugged from her lips alone. She tasted so damn sweet, perfect.

This was much better than his imagination. This was fucking real.

Cupping her hip for a second, he groaned at the

feel of her curves. She was all woman. Sliding his fingers underneath her shirt, he explored the skin of her stomach, moving up to cup her tits.

She pulled away. "No, too fast, too fast."

Instantly, he withdrew his hand even though his cock was in pain. He wanted inside her more than anything. Pulling away slightly, he kept his cock pressed against her pussy. He wasn't going to fuck her, but that didn't mean he couldn't enjoy being pressed against her.

"I'm sorry."

"It's okay. I shouldn't have kissed you back."

"I fucking loved it. Don't apologize," Gash said. He'd never take a woman unless she wanted him to. He liked rough sex, not fucking rape. Taking several deep breaths, he tried to calm his dick, which wasn't happening. He refused to move though. "We were fucking great together."

She smiled. "I thought so. I had nothing to compare it to…"

"Did I make it good for you?" he asked. He'd never been with a virgin in his life, and the last thing he even wanted to think about was believing he hurt her.

"At first it was painful. You were amazing, Gash. Even drunk you didn't hurt me." She strained against his hold, and he let her go. Charlotte touched his cheek. Her touch was hesitant.

"I fucked up when I didn't remember you," he said.

"You remembered me. You just didn't know it was me."

"If I'd known, I'd have never left without you."

"You're making yourself sound all alpha, like a book boyfriend."

"Huh?"

"Forget about it. It doesn't make any sense unless

you read." She tilted her head to the side.

Gash found her adorable.

"We're going too fast?"

"Just a little. I need to take a little time."

He pressed his rock hard cock against her. "I can wait for you."

"I expected you to be angrier with me," she said.

"Why?"

"Because we had sex, and I didn't tell you about it sooner."

Gash leaned down, taking another kiss. He was addicted to her lips. They were so fucking sweet. "We can't change what happened, and it's not going to define who we are. I'm looking forward." He smiled. "Besides, there's a lot more pleasure to be had. We don't actually have to fuck to get each other off."

She nibbled her bottom lip, which only served to drive him crazy. This woman had been right underneath his nose the entire time, and he was only now getting to know a taste. He wasn't going to give her the chance to get away from him. Their past wasn't a great one, but he was going to make sure their future was the best.

Briefly, he thought about Angel and Lash. He understood in that moment why the two worked. They were complete opposites, like chalk and cheese, exactly like him and Charlotte. Together, they actually made the perfect couple. What the fuck was he doing, thinking about another couple when he had Charlotte in his arms?

He slid his hand underneath her shirt, caressing over her stomach, then around to the center, to start flicking open the buttons. "I know exactly how to make you scream, baby, and to have this body coming apart."

"Gash?"

"That's right, moan my name. I'm not going to fuck you, Charlotte. What I'm going to do is let this body get used to my touch." Kissing down her neck, he sucked on her pulse before moving on to nibble on her collarbone. He flicked the last button open, exposing her chest. The black lace bra did little to cover her, and with a flick of the clasp at the front.

She moaned, and with another flick of his wrist, the bra was spread open. His mouth watered at her large red nipples. Leaning down, he flicked one tip with his tongue, before sucking the bud into his mouth. Cupping her other breast, he pinched the nipple, watching as it grew taut.

His dick threatened to burst the seam of his jeans he was so damn aroused. "You're so beautiful." Sucking the bud hard, he let it go a second later, gliding his tongue across her breasts, to give her other nipple the same attention. His dick pulsed some more, releasing some pre-cum into his boxer briefs. Closing his eyes, he groaned, thrusting against the bed before withdrawing from her. Kneeling between her thighs, he opened her jeans, and slid them down her thighs.

Her panties were lacy and matched the bra that she wore.

"I want you to trust me. I'm not going to step over the line, Char."

"I trust you."

He removed her panties, and stared down at her fuller body. Some men liked slender women where bones jutted through everywhere. Looking at her body, he loved her full tits, rounded stomach, and thick thighs.

Gash wasn't a small man, nor was he weak. He liked to grip onto a woman and fuck her hard, going as deep as he could go. Climbing off the bed, he removed his clothing, but even as he grabbed his aching cock, he knew he wouldn't fuck her today.

"Trust me."

"I do."

Slowly, he crawled between her thighs. He took possession of her lips before kissing down her body. Gash didn't take too much time at her breasts. He flicked each nipple before moving down, dipping his tongue into her belly button.

"What are you doing?" she asked.

"I'm going to have a taste of this pussy, baby. I've been thinking about it for some time, and I think it's only fair that I find out if it's as good as I remember."

Her pussy had a small dusting of pubic hair at the top. Settling between her thighs, he opened her naked lips.

"Why wax here, and not here?" he asked, stroking her pussy lips, then her pubic hair.

"I didn't want to feel like a child. I'm a woman, but I like to also be feminine," she said.

He was more than happy with that. His dick was especially happy.

Gash opened her lips and moaned at the sight of her swollen clit. She really was a beautiful, sexy woman. Flicking his tongue across her clit, he glided down to circle her cunt. She was soaking wet and started to thrust against him. He fucking loved it when she rubbed her pussy on his face.

The last thing he wanted was for his woman to not get off on being with him. He wanted it as badly as she did. His cock still leaked pre-cum all over the blanket as he licked her out.

"I want you, Gash."

"You've got me."

"No, I want this to be good for you, too." She pushed him away, going to her knees, and cupping his cheek. Her brown eyes were filled with heat. Just staring at her was turning him on. "There hasn't been anyone else for me." She slid her hand down his body to cup his cock.

"Baby, I can't say the same." He hated saying those words.

"I know you've fucked other women."

He covered her hand that was around his cock with his own. "There won't be any other women now, Char."

"You don't know that."

"I'm not a cheater." He'd witnessed the hell that Hardy had put himself and Rose through. He wasn't about to make the same mistake. "No more women, that's a promise."

He'd remain faithful for the rest of his life.

She slid her hand over his cock, and Gash couldn't help but love the fact no other man knew how damn perfect she was. No other man had known how big her tits were, or how tight her cunt was. Only him.

Gash had never considered himself a possessive man before, but with Charlotte in his arms, in his life, he could get used to the feeling. Sliding his fingers up the inside of her thigh, he teased her sweet pussy, pressing a finger inside her heat as he claimed her lips. Charlotte teased his cock, moving her hand up and down his length, arousing him further.

He could get used to this.

****

Whizz was printing some of the last pieces of information for Gash and Charlotte when the doorbell rang. He frowned, glancing over at Lacey who was reading her book. Quickly grabbing his cell phone, he saw that Lash had left him a message about thirty minutes ago that he was going to be around.

"It's Lash," Whizz said. "I'll go and answer it."

Leaving the nerd room, which was a name that

had certainly stuck, he opened the front door.

"What are you doing here?" Whizz asked, moving out of the way. The rain was coming in thick and fast. Lacey came out of the nerd room, and moved toward the supply closet where they kept spare towels in case of a downpour.

"I've come to ask you and Lacey something."

"Come on into my office," Whizz said, taking a seat at the computer. He closed the screens so he wasn't distracted with work to answer Lash's questions.

"What's going on, Lash?" Lacey asked. "Do you want a sandwich or anything?"

"God no," Lash said, holding his hand up.

"My cooking is not that bad!"

"No, it's worse."

Whizz chuckled, and Lacey did the same. They couldn't argue. Lacey's cooking was the worst.

"What brings you here?" Whizz moved to sit beside his wife, tugging her against his side. Lacey snuggled in close, and he stroked her arm. With Lacey in his arms, he felt he could take on the entire world, and win. Nothing could stop him providing he had her with him.

"Daisy."

"The little girl? Tabitha's friend?" Lacey asked.

"Yes."

"What about her?" Whizz asked.

"Angel wants us to adopt her, but the biggest problem at the moment is she's having a hard time with this pregnancy. She can't handle another child. Anthony, he's helping out where he can—"

"Wait? Is this Daisy with the addicts as parents?" Lacey asked, arms folded.

"Yeah. I had spoken to my lawyer about them before, and he looked into it. It seems Daisy's parents have always passed social services inspections. Their trailer, even though it's small, is still livable and safe to have a kid. The only thing my lawyer said I could do was to give them a talking to."

"Are you fucking shitting me right now?" Whizz asked. "They're addicts!"

"Tiny and I have talked with them, but they're not listening. Angel had to go and pick Daisy up from school, three hours after all the other kids left. I was talking with Angel, and we could adopt Daisy, and keep her away from those bastards."

"Why don't we just kill them?" Lacey asked.

"Because they're known, aren't they?" Whizz asked.

"Huh?"

Lash sighed. "Daisy is known to be friends with The Skulls. We could hide the bodies and shit, but you can guarantee it will fall back on the club."

"Great," Whizz said, snorting. "Fucking hate it when we turn the other way. We can't even beat the shit out of the fuckers without landing our asses in jail."

"So, do you have a plan?" Lacey asked.

"Yeah, I do." Lash pulled out an envelope. "Ned Walker knew a guy who was more than happy to take pictures, and they set a meet up. They're addicts all right."

"We're going to blackmail them?" Whizz asked, opening the envelope, and looking over the pictures.

"Why don't you just give this to social services?" Lacey asked.

"Simple, I give that shit to social services, they take Daisy, and she gets put into the system. I get them to adopt her to us, Daisy remains with us, and no one can do shit."

Whizz found a document at the back of the

pictures. Reading through, he looked up at Lash. "You want us to adopt Daisy?"

"What?" Lacey asked.

"Look, hear me out. I know you guys can't have kids, and I know you've adopted Sally, but I know you're also hoping to adopt again. Daisy, she's a good kid, a great kid who needs a good home. Please, give her a chance. If you don't want her, then me and Angel will take her. Angel wants to anyw—"

"We'll take her," Lacey said.

"Are we ready for that?" Whizz asked.

Lacey turned toward him. "Yes. Sally has been talking about us adopting another child. She's happy for us to add to our family."

Whizz had been in touch with the adoption agency, and they had warned it might be hard for them to find someone else. He'd had to pull a lot of strings for them to get Sally. Daisy would be a dream come true, even though he was about to surround himself with women.

"We'll do it."

"Do you want to come by tomorrow morning? We'll talk with Daisy, and my lawyer and I will go talk to them." Lash pulled out his wallet and handed them a picture.

Whizz looked over Lacey's shoulder to see a picture of Anthony, Tabitha, Daisy, Miles, Rachel, and Tate's Simon along with Devil's Simon. The next generation of Skulls and Chaos Bleeds. It was a picture of innocence, and Whizz couldn't help but smile. "They're all there."

"Not all of them. Markus isn't, and of course we've got more women that are pregnant. Angel gave me that picture, and she's got loads more. My woman loves taking pictures of everything."

"Thank you. Do you think Daisy will like us?" Lacey asked, her insecurity coming through.

"She's going to love us," Whizz said. "We can offer her a lot more, and we'll never forget to pick her up on time."

Lacey sighed. "Thank you, Lash, really, thank you."

"I'm just doing my job. I'm going to head back home. It's getting late, and I'm beat." Lash got to his feet, and leaving Lacey in his office, Whizz followed him out.

"What's going on?" Whizz asked.

"I've been on the phone to Devil. He told me that Master left them some evidence that he's been following them, and their women."

Whizz had been keeping updated on everything that was related to Master as it went back to Gonzalez, and back even further. For the past couple of years, The Skulls and Chaos Bleeds had been attacked by different clubs, organizations, with some of their pasts coming out to haunt them. Whizz himself had suffered for Zero's past. Lacey, she was part of the mess of Gonzalez, who'd torn her innocence from her, turning her into a ghost. Something wasn't adding up to him, and even though the enemy known as Master had left The Skulls alone, Whizz's gut was telling him it wouldn't be for long. Chaos Bleeds and The Skulls were linked. They had shared their time together in battle, and even though their friendship had been tested over the past couple of years, they would still fight for each other. Something wasn't right with Master, and Whizz kept his searching in private. He'd not told Lacey about what he was looking for. The last thing he wanted to do was concern her unnecessarily. Every time he thought he was on track to finding out who Master was, he always disappeared or

Whizz was blocked from locating anything more. Whoever Master was, he wanted his identity kept secret.

"Is he going to hit out at the old ladies?" Whizz asked.

"I don't know. Devil seems to think no one is safe, and I believe him." Lash ran fingers through his hair, looking perplexed. "I trust Devil. Whatever he needs, I'm going to makes sure the club will be there for him."

"Has he asked for anything specifically?" Whizz asked.

"A safe place for the women. He believes Master will come for them to get to the men." Lash looked pale. "I can't even believe I'm calling this man Master. I don't even know him, and already he's causing trouble."

"We attract trouble."

Lash nodded, releasing a sigh. "I'll catch you soon. I'll be doing church this Sunday, be there."

"Gash won't be there."

"I know. He's got his own shit to deal with. I'm sure we'll find out what's going on with him soon enough. Take care." They shook hands, slapping each other on the back.

Whizz stayed long enough to watch Lash leave his property. Closing the door, he pressed the code to the automatic gate, then locked every door and window into the house. He was going to protect his family. The same security system was at the club, and Whizz wouldn't let anything happen to The Skulls.

Chapter Eight

Charlotte opened her eyes and became aware of Gash cuddled up against her. She didn't freak out this time. They were both naked, and after the pleasure they had given each other well into the night, she didn't feel it was right to freak out. She had been with him every step of the way.

Biting her lip, she stared at his face. He was a good looking man. Seven years ago, he'd been good looking, a little thinner than he was now, but not as butch. He also hadn't had as many scars. There were cuts and scars over his body that she just knew were from his time in prison.

"You know, staring is rude," he said.

"I didn't even know you were awake."

He opened his eyes, and her heart rate sped up. She couldn't look away, nor did she want to. Gash was a handsome man. Her pussy grew slick recalling the way he held her down and brought her to orgasm. He was persistent in giving her pleasure, and she'd been too weak and too wanton to deny him.

"Do you like what you see?"

"Yes."

Gash stroked his hand up to cup her breast, and he pinched the hard nipple. He turned her so that her back was pressed against his front. His cock lay between the cheeks of her ass, and he was already swollen stiff.

"Last night, baby, that was just the beginning," he said, snuggling in close.

"It's after seven."

"Just five more minutes." He groaned, and Charlotte didn't want to pull away. She loved his arms around him and the way he held her. With him holding her, she felt like nothing could ever take that safety away.

He protected her.

After so many years of being alone, it was nice to have someone close, someone willing to fight for her. She'd never had that before.

Silence fell between them, but it wasn't a bad silence. It was peaceful. She closed her eyes, and he sighed.

"This is what I imagined," he said.

"Huh?"

"Waking up with my woman. Obviously, I always imagined that I'd be fucking my woman."

She giggled, slapping his hand. "Don't start."

"It's okay. I don't mind waiting. The anticipation is all part of it. Besides, you worked my dick many times last night. I doubt I've got any spunk left in me."

"Do you have to be gross?"

"Not being gross, baby. It's a club thing. I just say it like it is."

She rolled her eyes. "Will you ever tell me about what happened there?" she asked.

He tensed up. "Where?"

"Prison." She glanced behind her shoulder, and nodded. "You don't have to tell me about it. I just want you to know that I'm here if you need it."

Gash stayed quiet.

"The ward where I was had over twenty patients who were on suicide watch. I wasn't allowed to leave my room for about two months, unless I was in a wheelchair. They would take me to the dining room to eat, and someone would feed me. I had my own personal nurse who did everything."

He tightened his hold around her.

"Not being able to do anything made it worse. I

told Doctor Williams that him keeping me locked up with nothing to do just made me dwell on everything." She smirked. "It was the first time that I fooled him. He released me for twenty-four hours." She lifted her hand, showing the second faint line across her wrist. The first one she had done in the main hospital after attacking Jeff. The second was after manipulating the doctor. Each line, each scar, each mark, it told a story of her fight to leave this world.

Now, she was in Gash's arms, revealing parts of her life she had vowed to keep hidden.

"You don't have to talk to me about prison. I know what it's like to have everything taken away from you, and I just thought that you should know, I'm here." She licked her dry lips. "You know, in case you ever wanted to talk. I'm not saying that you should, but I'm here. I'm going to be quiet now."

Silence fell in the room, and she closed her eyes, wondering why the fuck she even opened her mouth.

"For the most part, there wasn't a problem while I was there. The club, Tiny, he made sure I had protection in there. There were times when protection wasn't enough."

"What happened?"

"Beatings and attacks." He gripped her hip, and moved her over, flipping her around. With him holding her hand, he placed it against his abdomen. "This is where I was pierced in the shower. It was quick, but I survived."

"How? I thought weapons weren't allowed."

"It doesn't mean that guards aren't paid to look the other way, and for the most part, they are. Other clubs, men, they can get paid to take men out, and being with The Skulls, I made a lot of enemies."

"Is that why you buffed up?" She touched his

arms, and her cheeks started to heat as she realized what she had said. "I mean, you're bigger than last time. I'm not really making this any better, am I?"

"You're sounding all right to me." He chuckled. "There's not a lot to do other than work out, read, and play. We all had jobs to do, but for the most part I figured the only way to survive is to keep strong. Tiny, he was there for me, and made sure when certain men got out, the club took care of them."

"They killed them?"

"To send a message. Fuck with a Skull on the inside, doesn't guarantee you're safe on the outside."

"What about the guards?"

"Another message. It took time, but my last year before it was found out that I wasn't the murderer, was the most peaceful of my life."

"Do you wish you could go back?"

"Fuck no. It was the worst place of my life. It was the worst, yet peaceful years there. That's all. I love being on my bike, being free to defend the club, and not having to worry about shit. I wouldn't trade that for the world."

There was a knock on the door.

"What is it?"

"I've got information for you," Whizz said.

In the next second the door opened, and Charlotte squealed, sinking more under the covers. She was naked.

"What the fuck, man?"

"If you weren't covered, you'd have told me to fucking hold on and come to the door. You're not, so tada." He sat down on the edge of the bed. "This is all the information you need. He has an apartment within the city. Jeff Wright was a dirty cop who also happened to be in league with Gonzalez and someone else. He's got his fingers in a lot of dirty pies, and because he's never been afraid to get dirty, a lot of people pay him a shit ton of cash to do it. There's even proof that he visited some of those men that attacked you in prison. Whoever it was, they were gunning for you, Gash."

Charlotte looked toward him to see that Gash didn't seem in the least bothered by that. She didn't understand it. Jeff wanted to hurt him, and someone was paying him to do it.

"What are you going to do?"

"Hunt him, kill him, and before that, find a way to get answers from him."

Whizz handed the file to Gash. "I have everything there. Rebecca and Jeff remained together after they went off the grid. They had new identities and killed of their current ones. As far as the world knows, Jeff and Rebecca died in a car crash seven years ago. It's funny, they died, and the next day, David and Tiffany appeared without much history around them. It was shoddy work. Enough to fool anyone who wasn't particularly looking, but not enough for me."

"How did you find that?" Charlotte asked.

"I'm paid to look through the cracks, and this was one big crack in their story. It was too much of a coincidence that you said David looked like Jeff in the image I brought up, then for him to own the apartment that was registered to Jeff. I'd be careful though, Jeff didn't have those funds to take you down, or to pay off the men. He's working for someone, and because of it, he got a big old payoff. I'm guessing whoever Rebecca was fucking, they were doing exactly the same."

"This is fucked up."

"Be careful. I've given this information to Tiny and also to Gash."

"Why?" Charlotte asked.

"Tiny was the Prez of The Skulls for most of the

last seven years. He handed over the reins a few months ago. When you go to kill a fucker from the past, it tends to bring some bad shit, believe me," Whizz said. "Are you making breakfast?"

Charlotte frowned. "Huh?"

"The food you cooked last night was amazing. I only get food like that when I visit the club or some of the old ladies when I see my brothers. When all of this is over, do you want a job? You can stay here. Have this room, and everything you want," Whizz said.

"What the fuck, Whizz? Stop trying to poach my damn woman," Gash said. "She's going to be staying with me."

Whizz chuckled, and Charlotte stared at him. The door closed, letting her know that Whizz had left the room.

"I'm staying with you?" she asked.

"Yeah. Do you really think I'm going to let you go? I don't have a place like this, but I've got a room at the club, and I've got the means to buy us a place." He cupped her cheek. "We were torn apart, and we didn't get a chance to be together."

"You want us to be together?" she asked.

Her heart started to pound, and Gash captured her lips. "Yes. We were going to have a baby. I can't change what happened to us, but I can change our future. You don't need to be going home alone ever again."

"You want me to be part of The Skulls."

"The Skulls is a family. It's not just some MC club that get together for sex and drugs. We've got a higher meaning, baby. We're a family, and you'd be part of that family. Lash, Angel, Whizz, Lacey, Tiny, Eva, I could go on and on with all the guys. You'd be my old lady."

"Really?"

"Yep. Just trust me, babe."

****

Gash stared down at the details where Jeff and Rebecca could be found. Whizz's warnings played through his mind.

"So, this is your car for the time being," Whizz said, handing him a set of keys. "Driving will be much better than a bike."

Staring at the keys, he raised his brow at Whizz. "I didn't think you agreed to me doing this," he said.

"I didn't agree to you going after Charlotte. I knew what she'd gone through. I saw the evidence that someone had tried to destroy. The good thing about everything going through the computer system, there's always something left for me to find, and I can dig it up. Paperwork is a lot easier to get rid of. You just burn the shit."

The mention of Charlotte's forced abortion twisted his gut. He was going to hurt Jeff, and it wouldn't matter what he did, Jeff would be getting off lightly.

"What is it?" Whizz asked.

"Nothing. I'm just thinking about all the ways I'm going to hurt that fucker."

Whizz looked back at the house where Sally and Lacey were hugging Charlotte goodbye.

"Do you really think she's going to kill Rebecca?" Whizz asked.

"I'm not going to let her. If I could, I'd leave her here, but she has a right to see this through." Gash watched as she tucked strands of hair behind her ear. She had left her hair down, and she looked so beautiful, innocent, even though she was anything but. Charlotte had been dragged into his world, and he was going to protect her. Lacey had lent her some jeans, which were a little loose. She also wore a white buttoned shirt. "I'm going to be the one to pull the trigger."

"Look, Gash, someone was out to get you nine years ago. Finding Jeff was close to Gonzalez and even The Darkness, and the men who tried to kill you inside—be careful."

"You don't think it was Gonzalez fucking with us back then?"

Whizz shrugged. "My gut is telling me to watch my back. Watch your own. I've got a feeling this isn't over, and it could get worse. That someone could still be out there hunting you."

"Hunting?"

"No one goes out of their way to cause this much chaos and just disappears. Do you have any enemies?" he asked.

Gash shook his head. "Well, I do have a brother, but he's probably dead."

"Brother? I didn't know you had a brother," Whizz said.

"A long time ago. He's been out of my life a long time."

"How long?"

"Fifteen years, maybe longer." He didn't give Andrew a thought as his brother wasn't worth his time.

"Wow, that's a long time not to know anything about family."

"He was an addict, and he couldn't take care of himself. He'd sell out the club rather than be loyal to it." Andrew had disgusted him, and when Tiny made the decision that Andrew was never going to make it in the club, he and Andrew had fought.

Charlotte came to stand next to him. "Are you ready?"

"Yep, we're driving, not riding," he said, showing the keys that Whizz had given him.

"Score." She hugged Whizz. "We'll see you soon."

Whizz pulled a cell phone out of his pocket. "It's programmed to have all The Skulls' numbers. Call anyone on that, and we'll come running."

Gash shook his hand, and opened the door, waiting for Charlotte to get inside.

"Don't do anything stupid," Whizz said. "If anything's out of place, leave. Don't get yourself killed because of possible bad information. I can only find out so much."

"I will. I won't let anything happen to her."

They shook hands again, and Gash walked around to the driver's side. He gave the gang a final wave, and started up the car.

"I packed us up some food so we don't have to make a stop."

"We'll drive toward this hotel," Gash said, pulling out a slip of paper. "I've already called ahead, and booked us both a room. We'll rest there, and then tomorrow morning, we'll take care of business."

"Do you have weapons?"

"Yes. This is Whizz's car, and he keeps them locked up in an inbuilt safe so no damage will come to them."

"Have I upset you?" Charlotte asked.

Frowning, he turned to her. "What?"

"You seem a little distant, and I was wondering if the reality of what has happened has dawned on you."

Gash shook his head. "No. I'm not upset about what I'm about to get you to do."

"What do you mean?"

"Look, killing someone, it takes its toll on a person."

"Rebecca and Jeff, I don't care what their names

are now. They deserve to die. Do you think I'm a bad person because I don't care?"

He glanced over at her, and saw that there was absolutely no expression on her face. She looked like they were talking about the weather rather than killing someone.

"How many people have you killed?" she asked.

"I don't keep count. With The Skulls, you learn to move on and forget about the shit that you do."

"When I first met you, I knew you were dangerous. Once I saw your leather jacket, I researched The Skulls. The club has a mixed bag for a reputation. You're dangerous and yet you fight to keep Fort Wills clean."

"It's our town. Tiny made sure all the bad shit stayed out." He'd been away when more trouble hit the club. The moment he got out, he'd promised Tiny he would wait to get his revenge until the club was in a better situation. "Does that bother you?" he asked.

"No."

"Seriously?" he asked.

"There's not a lot I can do about it. I take it you've never taken the life of an innocent before?" Charlotte asked.

"I can't guarantee anything."

"I attacked several male and female nurses while I was away in hospital," she said. "I hated how they kept me safe. It sucked."

Gash gripped the steering wheel. He didn't like how easily it came to her to talk about the fact she tried to end her own life. "How long has it been since you tried to end it?" He snapped the words out, and he looked toward her.

"It has been years, Gash. I've not tried for about two years. I decided to start living, not that you can call working and eating, really living."

"Does your doctor still talk to you?"

"Sometimes. He's always had a lot of patients."

"Did he pay careful attention to you?"

"No. Not at all." She reached out and took his hand. "I'm not going to blow or do something crazy. I had the therapy, and even though at times it's tough, I'm not going to do anything drastic. I'm good."

He held her hand as they drove forward. The long road out of Fort Wills was somewhat abandoned. There were a few houses dotted across the land, and plenty of farmland.

Tapping the steering wheel, he started to whistle. Relaxed and happy, Gash held onto Charlotte like a lifeline.

Within seconds, memories of the past started to flash through his mind.

"What can I help you with?" Rebecca asked.

"Well, baby, I'm here to see a slut about a guy," Gash said, taking a swig of his beer. This woman in front of him was just begging to be fucked. He saw the way she licked her bottom lip and the way she arched toward him. Her tits were practically exploding out of her shirt.

He shouldn't trust her, and he didn't, but he was on a mission to find his brother. Tiny had told him that he needed to locate Andrew. Gash hadn't given the fucker much of a thought, but if the club needed to know where he was, then he'd find him.

Most of the time in the past Andrew had been easily located in dives, drugs holes, or sex clubs. He was an evil fucker. Even when they were kids, Gash had known the evil that was in his brother's eyes.

Growing up in foster homes there had been rumors about Andrew. When they had found a place where a family wanted them both, Andrew had pretended to be the perfect son, but Gash had seen the way he commanded people. Women were scared of Andrew, and men flocked to him given how good he was at taking what he wanted.

Pulling out of the memory, Gash pulled up against the side of the road.

"What is it?"

"I was looking for my brother seven years ago," Gash said.

"Andrew?"

"Yes. Did I talk about him to you at all?"

"Not really. Whenever I asked you what you were searching for you always said a rumor."

Gash tapped the steering wheel repeating the same word. "Rumor. Rumor. Rumor."

"What's going on?"

"Andrew fought for a place within The Skulls. When we were growing up, he always believed he could do something better. He made everyone believe he was perfect, but he wasn't strong like the club needed. He couldn't hold his own in a fight, nor could he understand the meaning of the word loyalty." Gash laughed. "There had been rumors seven years ago of a guy who was plotting to end The Skulls, because of it, Tiny sent me out looking for my brother in case he'd give up any kind of information." Grabbing his cell phone, he climbed out of the car. "I've got to call Tiny."

"Okay."

Standing up, he pressed Tiny's number, and waited.

"Hello," a little girl said.

"Tabitha?"

"Yeah, you're not Simon."

Gash smiled. Tabitha and Simon, Devil's son, shared some kind of connection that drove both Devil and Tiny crazy. They were always trying to find ways to talk to each other. When Simon visited, he saw both of them holding hands, talking. It was sweet.

"No, honey, I'm not Simon. Is Daddy there?"

"If I go search for him, he'll know I took his phone. I'll get in trouble."

"Tell him he dropped it or left it in your room, or wherever you are. You shouldn't be taking his phone."

"He promised Simon would call him, and he'd give me the phone. Daddy lies sometimes. I know he doesn't like Simon." Tabitha sighed.

"He worries about you. You're what, five? You shouldn't be worried about shit like that."

"I'm nearly six, and you're not allowed to swear."

"Whatever, honey, you and I both know your dad says worse."

Tabitha chuckled. "Okey-doke."

He heard some noise in the background.

"Tab, I've told you not to take my phone," Tiny said.

"I didn't. You dropped it."

"Hello," Tiny said.

"She's so adorable."

"Yeah, adorable and sneaky." Tiny sighed. "What can I help you with?"

"Seven years ago. What were the true rumors going on at the club?" Gash asked.

"Shit. This is a long time ago. I had intel back then that someone was giving information about The Skulls. Secret shit about our drug runs, and our dealings with Ned Walker. The only person that I knew who could have that kind of information was your brother. Andrew, he wasn't exactly happy that he didn't make the cut. He left, and at the time we didn't have Whizz to keep an eye on him."

"You think Andrew was the one selling those rumors."

"I would, yeah, but then you got picked up for rape and murder, and after that shit, we were trying to keep you alive and safe, and shit returned to normal. There was nothing going on after you were sent down. We didn't have the means of finding out who was selling shit either."

"Yeah, and after I was sent down, the club had to deal with every kind of shit."

"You don't think that's a coincidence?" Tiny asked.

"No, not on your life. Something doesn't add up. Tell Whizz to look for Andrew. You know all the details."

Hanging up, he flicked his phone shut, and climbed into the car. "Did Jeff and Rebecca say anything to you?"

"Like what?"

"Anything at all. Simple shit."

"She told me she was seeing some rich guy who wanted her to do things for her. Sleep with certain guys. I never took all that much notice of her, or what she had to say. Jeff, he told me not to take offense. He was just doing his job. What's going on?"

"I don't know, but something doesn't add up, and I don't like it."

"What do you mean?"

He didn't know, and that was the problem. Gash only knew something was up.

Chapter Nine

Lacey was so nervous. Lash had driven out to their home to pick her, Whizz, and Sally up so that they could go and see Daisy. They were traveling toward Lash's house to see Daisy. The lawyer was already there, waiting for them.

Before they signed the papers, Lacey wanted to talk with Daisy to make sure the young girl was happy with it.

"Are you all right?" Whizz asked.

"I am." Lacey smiled, releasing a sigh. "Just nervous."

Sally leaned forward, gripping her shoulder. "She's going to love you."

Taking hold of Sally's hand, Lacey smiled at her. "Are you sure you're okay with this? I don't want you to think we're pushing you aside."

"You're not sending me back, and I'm not going to be selfish demanding that you can't help another person like me. Daisy's young, but she need us. I can't wait to be a big sister."

"We're going to be one wicked family," Whizz said.

"You'll have to read to her, and we're so going to have to go shopping," Sally said.

"What the fuck? You just want an excuse to spend my money." Whizz cursed, shaking his head.

Sally giggled. "You love us for it, and honestly, what else are you going to spend your money on? Laptops, tablets, phones?"

"I run a business."

"You're a nerd. A total nerd."

Lacey laughed, listening to Whizz and Sally

bicker. They cared about each other a lot. She knew that Whizz saw Sally as his daughter. At first, Lacey didn't think it was going to work between them as a family, but Whizz was different with Sally.

"A total nerd who can buy you exactly what you want."

"True."

They pulled into Lash's house and drove the car up the long drive. Climbing out of the car, Lacey linked her arms with Sally, and took Whizz's hand as they made their way to the door.

Angel opened the door. Her bright smile greeted them.

"It's so good to see you again," Angel said.

Out of all of the women in the club, Angel was the sweetest. Lacey couldn't even find the effort to find fault with the loving woman. When Lash had first taken over for the club, Lacey had had her doubts about Angel, but even with being the sweetest woman on earth, there was strength inside her.

Angel hugged all three of them, and glancing over her shoulder, she saw Lash there.

"What have I told you about hugging?" Lash asked, moving to his woman and pulling her against his side.

"They're a couple. Whizz doesn't mind," Angel said.

"Stop hugging everyone."

"He's possessive," Lacey said. Lash had always been particularly possessive of his woman, even from the start.

Angel rolled her eyes. "Come on. Daisy's eating breakfast with Anthony. They both slept in. I don't have a spare bed, so Daisy slept in Anthony's bed, topping and tailing. They're still young so I didn't think it would be too wrong."

Entering the house, Lacey couldn't help but smile. The whole house was charming, and feminine, exactly how she imagined Angel.

They made their way into the kitchen, which was a cook's dream. Angel was known for her ability to cook. Lacey hadn't been gifted with any kitchen skill at all. She even destroyed sandwiches.

Anthony and Daisy were sitting together, eating. Daisy wore Anthony's clothes, and Lacey's heart went out to her.

"The lawyer is waiting in the sitting room. Lash is just going to get him," Angel said. "Hey, Daisy, Lacey's here to see you."

The young girl looked up. Her brown hair was so long, and it fell around her. There was no care taken for it, and she didn't look loved at all. Lacey knew, deep in her heart, that she could love this young girl.

Anthony touched Daisy's shoulder, squeezing her.

Taking a seat beside the young girl, Lacey touched her hand. "Do you remember me?"

"Yes. You're Whizz's old lady, which is weird. You're not old."

Chuckling, she tucked some of that long hair behind her ear. "So, I've been talking with Angel and Lash, and we were thinking if you would like, you could come live with me and Whizz. What do you think about that?"

"Live with you?"

"Yes."

Lacey's heart was pounding. She didn't know what to do. What if Daisy didn't want to live with her and Whizz?

"In a real house?"

"Yes."

"You'll pick me up on time?"

"Yes. I wouldn't miss you."

"Come to school for events, and I can still be friends with Tabitha?"

"And me," Anthony said, glaring at Lacey.

"And Anthony?"

"Yes. You'll be a Skull child. Whizz and I, we'll take good care of you." Lacey squeezed her hand a little tighter, trying to gain comfort from her. She wanted to give this young girl a home. No one knew that she cared about Daisy and that it had grieved her each time she went back to her parents, who didn't care about her.

"Yes, I want that, please." Daisy climbed off her chair, and threw her arms around Lacey. "Please don't make me go back to the trailer and to Mom and Dad. They don't love me. They tell me every day."

Lacey's eyes filled with tears. No child should be told they were not loved.

Anthony climbed out of his chair and moved up behind Daisy, hugging her tightly.

"We'll love you," he said.

"I'll get everything resolved for you to come and stay with us, okay?"

"Yes."

****

Sally made her way out toward the back of Angel and Lash's house. She was the oldest of all of the kids, and even though she wasn't blood to the club, they treated her like she was. This was the first time she'd ever been part of a family, and with both Lacey and Whizz, Sally was able to heal.

There had been so many homes, so much abuse, some physical, some sexual, and a lot of mental.

Running fingers through her hair, she took a deep

breath. She loved being outside. There were times she would be locked in her room, and at some of the foster homes, they had bars on the windows.

She loved the outdoors.

Closing her eyes, she lifted her face to the sky and inhaled. There was no greater feeling than being outside, inhaling deep, and being relaxed.

"Penny for your thoughts."

She turned around, opening her eyes to find Steven leaning against the door, his arms folded as he stared at her. Sally hadn't even heard him leave the house.

"I didn't know you were here."

"I'm here to watch over you guys while Lash and Angel deal with Daisy."

"You're not a prospect."

She folded her own arms, fighting off the cold.

Steven sighed. "You're going to kill yourself if you don't cover up." He removed his leather jacket and moved toward her. He placed the jacket over her shoulders. "I don't want you getting cold."

"Thank you."

She pushed her arms through his, and the scent of him surrounded her. Her cheeks started to heat, and she turned away from him. The last thing she wanted him to know was that she liked him. Steven was really sweet to her. She'd seen him with other women, and he was never sweet to them.

"I could have taken care of everyone," she said.

"You could, and you'll be making lunch for us all. You belong to the club, Sally, and I protect what belongs to The Skulls."

Nodding, she wouldn't look at him. In all of her life she'd never once had a crush on anyone. Steven was the first man that she'd ever felt anything for. He was older than she was by fifteen years, and she wouldn't ever act on her feelings. He probably only saw her as a stupid kid.

"Are you okay, Sally?" he asked.

"Yeah, why?"

"You're quiet."

"I'm just enjoying the fresh air."

"Do you have any homework to do?"

"No."Glancing over her shoulder, she smiled at him. "I'm good."

He nodded, and turned to go inside to the kitchen. The moment he left, her heart felt heavy. She didn't understand it.

Steven was just a guy, and she wasn't going to let her feelings for him get in the way.

****

Closing the door, Steven hesitated. Sally was different. When she first was adopted by Lacey and Whizz, she'd been closed off, but once he proved to her that he wouldn't hurt her, she'd opened up. Now once again, she was closed off.

"Why do you look like someone has taken your favorite toy?" Lash asked.

"I thought you were going?"

"Heading out now." Lash looked behind him. "She's wearing your jacket. She's fifteen years old."

"Ew, what the fuck? She was cold."

"You do know she's got a huge crush on you, right?"

Steven froze. "What?"

"Yep. Lacey and Whizz know it as well."

"I would never do anything like that. She's not old enough—"

"We know that. Just be careful with her. I don't want to have Whizz trying to fucking kill you. I'd miss you. Maybe when she's older."

Steven shook his head. "No. She's not my type. She's not a club whore, and I'm not good enough." Looking back toward Sally through the window, he saw she had taken a seat on the steps. He noticed she did that a lot, spent hours sitting outside staring at the stars, or the sky.

"I never thought I'd be the kind to settle down and have kids. I didn't even see past fucking the next available pussy. Seeing Angel, and getting to know her, I wouldn't change a single thing about the way my life has gone with her. She's the love of my life, the very reason I wake up in the morning."

"Why are you telling me this?"

"One day, Sally will leave the club and go away to college. She'll grow up, and when she returns, she'll no longer be just some girl, and you may not even be the same guy. Don't throw away a chance because it scares you."

"She's fifteen."

"She won't always be fifteen." Lash shrugged. "Keep your hands away from her."

Steven watched as Lash made his way out of his own home. The kids were set up in the front room, and there was a gate keeping them there, not that it worked. The kids could wander around whenever they wanted as they knew how to open the gate. They were good though, and would come to him if they needed anything.

Entering the kitchen once again, he saw that Sally was standing near the counter by the stove. She'd left his jacket on a chair and was reading a book.

Just be yourself.

"I don't have a crush on you," Sally said, glancing up at him.

"Huh?"

"You didn't shut the door properly. I heard everything. Don't worry, I'm not going to try and jump your bones or anything."

"You don't have a crush."

Sally looked over the edge of her book. She shook her head. "No."

Steven would never understand why he was a little bit gutted at that information. There was seriously something wrong with him. Sally was too damn young, and he only fucked women who knew there wasn't going to be anything between them.

He and Sally didn't stand a chance.

Chapter Ten

Later that day

After driving all day, and only stopping to use the toilet or to get some food, Gash was tired. He left Charlotte at the hotel while he drove to the nearest Chinese takeout for food. They had spent the whole day talking, and he'd remembered everything that he once used to know about Charlotte. He remembered that her favorite color was blue; she hated tofu, and loved listening to pop music.

Gash smiled remembering one day when he entered their apartment, Rebecca hadn't been there, but he'd stood and watched Charlotte. The music had been so loud that no one would have been able to think. Charlotte had been dancing around the whole apartment, singing at the top of her voice. It was one of the rare moments when he caught her without Rebecca waiting around. Charlotte was usually open and relaxed, but he'd noticed she was a little colder when Rebecca was around.

He'd watched her, unable to look away. She stirred his cock and twisted his gut with how sexy she had looked. Her tits had been bouncing, and the clothes she'd worn hadn't covered up those curves, and he'd wanted her.

When she turned toward him, the smile that she greeted him with had had feelings awakening within him. She had danced toward him, grabbing his hands, and tugging him into a dance. The temptation to kiss her had been so strong that he'd started leaning in toward her when the door opened, interrupting them. Rebecca had come back to the apartment, and Gash had wanted her to disappear so that he could spend more time with

Charlotte. That was part of how he remembered his time with her, always wanting more, and never getting it.

There had been moments through prison that not only his desire for revenge had kept him going, nor the memories of the mystery woman, which he now knew to be Charlotte. It was the memory of the fleeting times he'd spent with her outside of a bedroom. He'd not known she was the woman he'd spent one amazing night with.

Closing the car and locking it, he made his way toward their room. Stepping inside after he unlocked the door, he secured them in for the night, and glanced out the window to make sure no one had followed them.

As he turned back toward the room, Charlotte stepped out of the bathroom, covered in a towel.

"Hey," she said, holding the towel against her breast. There was a little slit up the side of her thigh, exposing some of her flesh. Fuck, his cock went rock hard.

"Hey," he said.

"You got some food."

He licked his lips. The only thing he wanted to eat was standing in front of him. All he wanted to do was push her to the bed, spread her thighs, and lick that sweet cunt. She was sweet as well. He'd only had a little taste, but he wanted another one.

Placing the food on the floor, he shoved the key into his pocket. His cock pressed against the front of his jeans, begging to get out.

"Drop your towel," he said.

"What?"

"You heard me. Drop your towel."

Charlotte stared right at him, her knuckles going white where she gripped the towel. "You bought food."

"I did, and we'll eat it soon. It's too hot. Drop

your towel."

He removed his leather jacket, and tugged his shirt over his head. Kicking his boots off, he stared at her, waiting. Looping his fingers through the rings of his jeans that held his belt, he watched.

"I'm not going to wake up in the morning and forget. I'm here, right now. Don't you want to take a chance?"

She licked her lips, and finally dropped her gaze to stare down his body. He saw the moment she caught sight of his dick as her eyes grew wide.

Opening his jeans, he pushed them down his thighs, careful when he released his cock. He stood before her naked, and stroked his dick. "You see what you do to me, baby." Coating his fingers in the pre-cum, he worked the liquid down his shaft, getting him nice and slick.

Seeing the conflict in her eyes, he bent down, and pulled out several condoms from his jeans. "I bought them. There was a pharmacy near the Chinese, and I figured it would make sense to have them."

"You're that sure of yourself."

"I know I want you, and from what I remember, you want me. Don't deny your pussy is soaking wet. We both know it is."

"You're being arrogant again."

"No, I know what we both want. You're too busy denying it."

"I'm not denying anything."

"One day, we'll have kids but not yet. We've got a lot of stuff to do together first."

"You think we're going to have kids?"

"Yeah, lots of them. Once this is done, we're going to get married, have some time together, and get started on six kids."

"Six?"

"You keep repeating everything I say," he said.

"Do you even hear yourself?"

Gash smirked. "I hear myself. Tell me what I've just said isn't a dream come true for you?"

"I've not thought about it."

He saw it was the truth. Charlotte wasn't trying to lie to him.

Closing the distance between them, he cupped her face, tilting her head back. "All of these years it has been you that has brought me back from the brink of going insane. When I got out of prison I didn't know what I was missing, but being with you, I don't want this to end, Charlotte."

She snorted. "You thought I helped send you away."

"Yeah, and there's nothing I can say to express how sorry I am about that. I was conflicted, but I'm not conflicted anymore. I know what I want, and I want you."

"You want me?"

"Yeah. You're my old lady, Charlotte. There's not going to be another woman for me, and there's going to be no other guy for you but me." He stroked his thumb over her bottom lip. "We didn't get our chance last time. *This* is our chance, and I'm not going to back down without a fight." He pressed a kiss to her lips. It was a gentle kiss, nothing too demanding. "We're going to have kids someday, and you're going to have my ring on your finger."

Charlotte chuckled. "You're so sure of yourself."

"Drop your towel. Take a chance with me, and let me show you that I mean every single word I say."

She paused, the smile dropping from her lips.

"I'll take care of you. I'll love and protect you."

"Love?"

"Yeah, love, Charlotte."

"You don't know if you love me. It has been too soon."

Gash sighed. She was always so doubtful. He didn't remember her being like this. From the night he first saw her, he'd come to the realization that he was in love with her, had always been in love with her. Over seven years ago, he'd fucked her roommate, and throughout it all, he'd imagined it was Charlotte underneath him. She was the only woman he wanted, the only woman that had invaded his heart, and settled there. No matter how much he wished to deny it, being around her again, he couldn't do it. They were meant to be together.

"Give me a chance to prove myself to you. No more pain."

She was his entire world.

If she asked him to turn around now, and spend the rest of their lives together, he would. He would forget about his need for revenge, and live the rest of his life without it. Charlotte gave him a future that he could settle with forgetting his past.

Charlotte dropped the towel, and he wrapped his arms around her, gripping her ass, and pulling her close to him. His cock pressed against her stomach, and he ran his hands up and down her body. Her pale skin was so soft.

"You've got a lot of scars."

He pulled away, sliding his fingers down her arms, and turning her wrists up. "So do you." Gazing down her body, he saw there were scars on her body as well. Across her stomach, there was an uneven scar. Caressing his fingers across the scar, he frowned. There was another on the other side of her stomach. He looked down to find another scar on her thigh. "What did you do?"

"I sucked at taking out my wrists, so I tried other ways, bleeding out. Doctor Williams was so annoyed. I almost succeeded with my thigh. After that, he kept me in confinement, and made sure I couldn't move. He talked to me, and I didn't have a choice but to listen to him. It was the best thing he ever did for me."

"No more."

"No more." She nodded.

Going to his knees, he pressed a kiss to each scar on her stomach, then on her thigh. Next, he kissed her wrists. "Forgive me for not being with you."

"There's nothing to forgive, Gash."

Climbing to his feet, he kissed each of her nipples then sank his fingers into her hair. Slamming his lips down on hers, Charlotte gasped, opening her lips. Sliding his tongue into her mouth, he moaned, loving the way she gave herself to him.

"You've had no other man since me?" he asked.

"Not one. I've not been interested."

He pressed her against the wall, releasing her hair, and putting her hands above her head. "I can't promise this time will be slow. Soon, I'll go slow, not today."

"I didn't ask for slow."

"I was fucking wrong about you, so wrong." Claiming her lips once again, Gash held her hands up against the wall with one of his, and with his other hand, he caressed down her body. He pinched her right nipple, pebbling it. Down he went to slide his hand between her thighs. He cupped her pussy, teasing her clit. She was soaking wet.

Moving his hand down, he slid two fingers into her wet cunt.

"Do you want my dick, baby?"

"Yes."

"I'm going to give it to you, and make you beg, and scream my name."

She moaned.

He stroked his thumb against her clit, teasing her even more.

Charlotte moaned, and her cream coated his fingers inside her. He pumped in and out, finding a pace that took her to the edge of pleasure and kept her there.

She was responsive.

Capturing her lips, he glided his tongue inside her mouth, and she met him stroke for stroke.

Her body thrust onto his fingers, and he wanted to feel her coming on his fingers. Tonight, he wasn't in a rush to have this over. They had seven years, and a lot of pain to get over.

"Come for me, Charlotte. Soak my fingers with your cream."

She groaned as he spread his fingers, opening her up. Charlotte was so tight that he needed to stretch her to accommodate him.

His cock pulsed, spilling pre-cum against her stomach. This wasn't about him, but about her.

He flicked his thumb from side to side, and Charlotte came apart. Her orgasm spilt onto his fingers. Gash didn't stop. He slowed down his strokes until she was still gasping his name.

When it was over, he removed his fingers from her pussy, and sucked the digits into his mouth.

"You taste so damn good, baby," he said. He released her arms, and she wrapped them around his neck, holding onto him.

She sighed. "That was amazing."

"There's more to come."

****

Part of Charlotte knew this was crazy, but another part knew it was the right thing to do. She wanted to be with Gash, and being in his arms, settled the war within her. He'd never hurt her, and apart from grabbing her around the throat, he never had.

There hadn't really been much pain then either. He'd caught her by surprise more than anything.

Gash took possession of her mouth, and he moved them toward the bed. She kissed him back with a passion that startled her. Charlotte had never considered herself to be particularly into sex. Gash was awakening all of her body, making her crave his touch in the most basic way.

He dropped her to the bed, and she stared up at him. Gash reached down, grabbing one of the condoms. "We deserve this chance to be together. No kids yet."

"No kids yet." It didn't hurt anymore. Seven years it had taken, and Gash being back in her life for her to finally get over it.

"We will, baby."

"Yes."

He tore into the condom and slid the latex over his cock.

She opened her thighs as he climbed onto the bed, and he settled over her.

"Do you want me to turn back and head to the club?" he asked.

Charlotte frowned. "Jeff? Rebecca?"

"I can live without taking them out. I've got you, and they can't take that away from me. Tell me if you want me to leave and we'd start our life together."

She cupped his cheek. "You'd do that for me?"

"Yes. I'd do that for us. No questions asked."

Stroking her cheek, she ran her finger against his

lip. Charlotte struck, grabbing his shoulders, and pushing him to the bed. She straddled his waist, and then was nervous about her weight. "Am I too heavy?" she asked.

He shook his head, grabbing her hips, and grinding against her body. They were not having sex yet, but his desire was evident. "You'll never be too much for me." He ran his hands up her body, cupping her tits. She moaned as he fingered her nipples, pinching them.

Taking hold of his hands, she placed them beside his body.

"You don't like my hands on your tits?"

"I like it a lot, but I've got something more to say and do first. Leave your hands there." She waited until he sighed and relaxed beneath her touch. Releasing his hands, she stared down his body. There were scars that decorated his body. Some of the scars were covered by the ink that he'd decorated his body with. Starting at his neck, she found the first scar across his collar bone. Tracing her fingers over each mark, she tilted her head to the side, staring down his body. "Your body is covered in scars. Some of those were given to you because you're a Skull, right?"

"Yes."

"Others were given to you in prison?"

"Yes."

She saw the uneven ones, and guessed they had to be made from an object not generally used to cut flesh. "Did they hurt?"

"Yeah, but I got them back, and if I didn't, then the guys did when they were released."

"The Skulls took care of you?"

"Yes."

"I like that." She stroked down his rock hard stomach. "I like to know that you were taken care of by people who cared about you."

"No one cared about you."

"I wasn't important, Gash."

He sat up, gripping her arms. At first she gasped, flinching as he moved so fast, then feeling stupid. "I would never hurt you, Charlotte. You're important to me, and back then you were, too."

"I want you to kill them, Gash. They ruined our lives, and what if they come back to destroy us again?" She pressed a kiss to his lips, and her eyes filled with tears. "I'm a bad person."

"No, baby, you're not."

"What we're doing, it's not wrong?" she asked.

"It's wrong, but I don't give a shit about wrong. Rebecca, she brought Jeff into our life. He stole our child from us, and our future. We need to have a little payback, and I need to know that he's never going to come back to hurt us."

"Then I don't want to turn around and head back. We both came here to do something, and we're going to get it done."

He cupped the back of her head, claiming her lips.

Closing her eyes, she held on tightly to Gash as he flipped her to her back, pressing her to the bed. Opening her thighs wide, she watched as he pulled back enough to grip his cock. He aligned the tip to her entrance, and then he was sliding inside her.

She couldn't help the wince as he wasn't a small man. He was large all over, and it had been so long since he'd last been inside her. Her body was greedy for more, wanting him inside.

He captured both of her hands, locking them either side of her head.

With one sharp thrust, he plundered her, going to the hilt within her. She cried out, unable to hold back the bite of pain as he fucked inside her.

Gash paused for a second, pressing his head against hers. "I don't want to hurt you."

"It's okay. It's, erm, it's been a while."

"I'll get you used to my touch, baby." He claimed her lips, and she gave everything to him. "You're so fucking beautiful."

He broke the kiss to move down to take one of her nipples into his mouth. She couldn't lie still as the arousal got stronger. Gash had already brought her to orgasm once, and she was ready for a second. Thrusting her hips up, she took him deeper. The pain was gone, and the pleasure heightened her senses.

"Let me hear you scream, baby," he said, whispering the words against her ears.

"Yes, please, Gash."

"Tell me to fuck you, Charlotte. Tell me you can take my cock, and love it."

"Fuck me, Gash. Please, fuck me."

He released her hands and went to his knees, grabbing her hips. Gash pulled out of her only to hold her where the tip of his cock was inside her.

"Look at me, Char," he said.

Staring into his eyes, Charlotte couldn't look away even if she wanted to, not that she did.

"I want you to look at me so that you know who is fucking you, taking you, and loving every second of it. I love your body, Char. I love that you're strong, and that we're together now."

Every word he said tore down the doubt that she once had. He wasn't going to hurt her, nor was he going to leave her, not once.

"Fuck me," she said.

"Do you believe me?"

"I believe you."

He slammed all the way inside her. Gash didn't stop for her to get accustomed to the feel of his cock. He took, and she gave him with abandon, and loved every single second of it. Not a moment went by that she didn't love it. He fucked her harder, going deeper than before.

"Yes, please, yes," she said, screaming his name.

Gash pounded inside her. He ran his hands up and down her body but didn't stay in one place. Touching her pussy, he slid his fingers across her clit, then spread the lips of her pussy open. She watched his thick cock disappear inside her only to reappear. The condom was covered in her cum.

"Do you see us together, babe? See how damn good we look."

He fucked inside her harder, going deeper still.

"Yes."

"This is how it's always going to be with us, baby. I'm going to fuck you every single chance I get, and it's going to be fucking amazing. My woman, my old lady, my wife, and I'm not going to stop. I'm going to own you."

She loved every single word he said.

"You feel so fucking good."

The only sounds in the room were of their heavy breathing, and their flesh slapping together.

The pleasure was out of this world.

"Come for me, Char, let me feel you come on my dick."

He fingered her clit, stroking her. Charlotte didn't think she could come a second time, but he proved that wrong as he continued to fuck her at the same time as teasing her pussy.

She came apart in his arms, and he rode her harder still.

Only when she came down from the peak did he

let her go. This time he let her go, grabbed her hips, and started to ride her harder, fucking her deeper.

Charlotte screamed his name, loving the feel of him inside her. He slammed deep within her, and staring into his eyes, she watched as he came hard, filling the condom. She felt his cock pulse with each jet of his cum, and yes, she was pleased that he had in fact used a condom.

He collapsed over her, and she didn't mind his weight, wrapping her arms around him.

"Was that better than last time?" he asked.

She couldn't help but laugh. "Yes, it was much better."

****

"You think he's coming?" Tiny asked. He looked into his dining room that had several Skulls seated around the table. The club was his family, and Eva loved cooking for them all, even with their latest child. He was pleased it wasn't another set of twins. Miles and Tabitha threatened to send him to an early grave.

"It's only a matter of time, Tiny. I don't have a clue who this guy is, and I don't know what to fucking do. I'm a father now, a husband. I can't just let shit happen, and hope for the fucking best that I make it out alive," Devil said.

Tiny had been talking to Devil on and off for the past couple of months. He was trying to repair the damage that he had caused between the two clubs. The way he'd dealt with Devil was one of the reasons he handed the club to Lash. It was time for him to move on, and when he started The Skulls, he'd promised himself that he would find the right man to take over. Lash was that man, even if he didn't believe it at times, but he was doing a great job. Tiny couldn't fault him. Taking on The Skulls wasn't easy, and anyone who thought so didn't understand the role that was being handed to them. It wasn't easy. The lives of men, women, and children were in your hands.

"We know fuck all about this bastard, Tiny."

Rubbing at his eyes, he watched as Eva laughed at something Rose said.

Hardy, Rose, Tate, Murphy, Kelsey, Killer, Zero, and Prue were at his table tonight. He watched as his youngest daughter Tabitha talked with his oldest daughter, Tate. Those two were alike in a lot of ways. Tabitha hadn't inherited Tate's bitchy attitude though, which he was thankful for.

There was only so much he could take with his daughter. He'd been forced to make Murphy stand up, and to put her in her place. The Skulls wasn't for his daughter to stick her nose in.

"Lash is creating a safe place for you. Whenever you're ready, come here, and we'll fight this person together."

"Whizz hasn't found anything out?"

"He's working on it, but like I said, whenever he gets close, he hits a dead end."

"We believed he was a businessman," Devil said. "That doesn't help?"

"No. Master is a businessman, only his business isn't exactly kosher. He buys girls, but we believe he also sells them. There are possible connections to known drug lords and cartels. Nothing concrete, but speculation."

"You're shitting me?" Devil asked.

"Whizz is doing the best he can."

"I know. Fuck, I know. I can't let anything happen to Lexie. She's the love of my life. Her and my kids."

"There's always a place here for you." He stared at Eva, and his family. They were his life, and he would do whatever it took to keep them safe.

"I've got to go. I'll talk to you soon when we know more."

Tiny nodded, closing his cell phone. This shit with a fucker known as Master was starting to get out of hand. He'd given Whizz the information he needed to find out about Andrew.

"What's going on?" Eva asked, coming toward him.

He shook his head. "I need to make a phone call."

"Tell me what's going on." Eva stood in front of him with her hands on her hips. Fuck, he loved her so much, and she was so damn sexy, she made him ache. This woman had enriched his life and given him something to fight for. Before her, there was nothing else, and he didn't want anything else but her.

"Master, he's hitting out at the Chaos Bleeds women. He's threatening them, and we can't find anything, Eva. Whizz says he's like a ghost. We can't find him, and if we can't find him, we can't fight him."

Eva wrapped her arms around him. "We'll get him."

"How?"

"I don't know, but someone like that can't stay hidden for long. You've just got to give him time to either screw up, or come out and play."

Tiny held the back of her head, leaning down he captured her lips. "I love you, baby."

"I love you, too. We're in this together, you and I."

"I suppose Tab will stop moaning about Simon visiting again if he's here."

Eva chuckled. "You're just going to have to accept the fact our daughter loves a Chaos boy."

Tiny smiled. "We'll see."

Chapter Eleven

Gash stroked the length of Charlotte's back, and felt complete. They had finished off the Chinese food, and after that, they'd snuggled up together.

He took hold of her hand, staring down at their locked fingers. "This is how it would have always been."

Charlotte sighed. "I wish we'd have been together."

"Me too." He'd have given anything to change the last seven years. They could have a family now, and he'd have been more than happy to come home to her every night.

"What happens when we get back?" she asked.

"We're going to marry."

She gasped, looking up at him. "Seriously?"

"Yeah. We've wasted enough time, and I know I'm not going to change my mind." He kissed the top of her head. "I love you, Charlotte."

He noticed she didn't say it back to him.

"I can't—"

Silencing her protest with a kiss, he wasn't interested in hearing her doubts. He knew she'd have them. "I don't need to hear the words." The fact she hadn't been with anyone else since him was all he needed to know. Charlotte loved him. She just wasn't ready to commit again, not that he blamed her.

Pushing the blanket from them, he kissed down her throat, nibbling on her collarbone. He didn't stop there. The light cast from the lamp gave him the perfect view of her body. Taking one of her nipples between his teeth, he nipped her bud before sliding his tongue across the valley of her tits, toward her other. He paid each tit careful attention, before trailing his tongue down her stomach, dipping into her belly button.

"Gash?"

"I've got you, baby." Opening her thighs, he spread the lips of her pussy, stroking his fingers across her clit. "You're so sweet and wet. Your body knows that you belong to me, Charlotte. Don't fight it."

In answer, she groaned.

"Please," she said.

Moving down, he pressed his tongue to her clit, tasting her cream. He was already addicted to her taste, and he'd never grow tired of licking her pussy. Flicking her clit, he glided down, plunging his tongue into her cunt.

Her cunt tightened him. Fucking her with his tongue, he caressed her clit with his fingers.

Gash got her nice and wet, then gripped her hips, flipping her onto her knees. She released a scream.

"I've got you, baby." Grabbing another condom, he tore into the packet, rolling the latex over his dick. He pressed the tip to her entrance and slowly slid inside her. "When we get home, I'm going to make you watch me take you like this, fucking inside you. I love watching you, Charlotte." He stared down at where his cock was inside her. "Such a pretty tight pussy." Unable to help himself, he slapped her ass, gripped her hips, and pounded inside her. She was just so perfect.

There was no other word for it. Charlotte was perfect for him.

Running his hands up her back, he gripped her hair, wrapping it around his wrist, and lifting her up so that her back was pressed against his. The angle meant he couldn't get as deep inside her as he wanted, but that was okay. He was a patient guy. With his free hand, he cupped her cheek, forcing her to turn toward him to look at him.

He claimed her lips once again. Sliding his hand down, he cupped her breast. She opened her mouth, and he plundered her lips. She covered his hand with her own, and he touched her pussy, stroking her clit. She arched against his touch.

"I always dreamed it would be like this," she said.

"You dreamed about me?"

"Yes. You were always there. I couldn't get away from you, and I didn't want to."

He liked that. Easing her down to the bed, he kept one hand between her thighs, touching her clit. Gash moved his fingers down to feel himself sliding inside her. He had a lot of plans once they were done, and he wasn't going to stop until Charlotte was owned by him. Gash wasn't a foolish man. He knew what was precious to him, and this woman was it. She was his lifeline, the person he'd been waiting for.

Pounding his dick inside her tight heat, he groaned, loving the way she squeezed him tight. When they were ready, he was going to take her without a condom, and be reminded of how good she felt underneath him. He fingered her clit, feeling each clutch of her cunt as she tightened around him. It was the best feeling in the world. She was the best pussy he'd ever been inside. This must be what all the other brothers felt when they settled down, content, happy, and ready to fuck their woman at a moment's notice.

"Gash," she said. "Please, I need you."

"You're going to come for me, baby?"

"Yes." She screamed his name again, and he pinched her clit hard.

Her cunt went tighter than a fucking vise as she clenched his cock.

"Fuck," he said. The pleasure was out of this world, and once she came down from her own release, he gripped her hips and pounded inside her. He watched his cock fill her pussy, the way she sucked him inside. Slamming deep within her, he gripped her hips so tight that he knew it was going to bruise. His marks on her skin were exactly what he wanted. She was his woman, and he wanted everyone to know it.

Gash fucking loved her, and it wasn't a revelation that surprised him. He accepted that, relished it, and it wasn't going to stop. This was the kind of love that he'd seen between Angel and Lash, Eva and Tiny, all of The Skull couples.

Leaning over her, he bit her shoulder, and thrust inside her one final time, filling the condom. One day soon he was going to be filling her pussy and watching his cum spilling from her lips.

Wrapping his arms around her, he squeezed her tight as the pleasure consumed his entire body.

"You're fucking beautiful," he said.

Turning on his side, he kept hold of her, kissing her neck, and stroking her body.

"I could stay like this forever," she said. "You know I never thought I'd see you again."

"When I got out, I was going to come looking for you. The club, they needed me first."

She stroked his arm. "From what I've seen of your club, I love it."

"You'll have to quit your job."

"What will I do?"

"There's always something to do at the club, and we're starting up some new businesses. We've got a gym planned, which will need some people to run it. There's a beauty shop that Angel suggested."

She chuckled. "I'll find work. I couldn't just sit around waiting for you to come home."

"That's not the way our club works. I'm not

saying every single club works like ours. Each MC is different. The Skulls, for the most part is a family club."

"You're saying there's no screwing going on?"

Gash laughed. "Yes, there's a lot of screwing. We're a bunch of guys, but when the families are in, that shit is nowhere to be seen."

"It seems hard to believe. A tame biker club."

"We're not fucking tame."

She turned her head, and he saw she was smiling. "I'm just teasing you. I know The Skulls all mean business."

"How?"

"Sometimes I'd read newspaper clippings about what happened in Fort Wills. Our night together, you told me that was where you lived."

He'd never told anyone that, not even Rebecca. "I told you a great deal, didn't I?"

"Not a lot. You didn't tell me why you were seeing Rebecca." She paused, and her body went tense. The tightening of her body squeezed his dick, and he groaned.

"I've got to take off the condom," he said, tapping her thigh. He eased out of her, and removed the condom, throwing it in the trash before sliding back in, wrapping his arms around her. "Why did you go tense?"

"That night we were together, you spoke of your feelings for me." She looked up at him, and her cheeks were red. "You told me how much you liked me, that you thought I was beautiful, and even though Rebecca thought she was better than me, it wasn't the case." Tears once again filled her eyes. "You told me that if you weren't so busy, you'd have tried to make me yours forever."

"I knew who you were?"

"Yes. It was only in the morning that you forgot

who I was."

"I didn't mean for shit like that to happen," he said.

"I get that now. I always blamed myself. You were drunk, and I knew you wouldn't remember. Well, I hoped you would, but when you woke up, I knew that you didn't have the slightest idea of who I was."

Locking their fingers together once again, Gash sighed. "Everything fucked up around us."

"What were you looking for back then?" she asked.

"My brother. Tiny wanted me to make sure he wasn't causing any trouble."

"Did you ever find your brother?"

"No."

Charlotte didn't say anything more about that. Minutes passed, and he held her tightly against him.

"Gash?" Charlotte asked.

"What, baby?"

"Will we be okay?"

"Yes, you can count on it."

****

The following day, Charlotte stared up at the large building that was supposed to house Jeff and Rebecca. Glancing down at the piece of paper that Gash had given her, she looked at the large building. "Are you sure about this?"

"I'm more than sure."

"Jeff and Rebecca weren't wealthy."

"It makes you wonder who they were working for," Gash said.

She stared at the man who had stolen her heart within hours of being in her life once again. Seven years ago, he'd come into her world fucking another woman, and she had fallen for him just as easily. What was it about Gash that she was too weak to walk away from?

Last night, she had fallen asleep in his arms, happy and safe. Throughout the night, he woke her up to make love, and fuck her. He alternated between taking her hard and slow. She loved every second of it. His cock was so big, and he knew what to do with it. After seven years of not being with anyone, Gash had awakened her once again.

"You think someone else is behind what happened back then?" Charlotte asked.

"Seeing this shit, I'm convinced of it." He pulled into the underground parking, typing in the code that she imagined Whizz had given to him.

They pulled up, and Charlotte took a deep breath.

"Are you okay?" he asked.

"Yeah, everything is just—yeah, I'm okay. It just seems pretty surreal is all."

You're about to go and kill a man and a woman.

A woman you agreed to kill.

You're going to watch him take another man's life.

She thought about Jeff and Rebecca, her memories going back to that moment in the hospital when she realized what had been taken from her. The pain was still there, but she could finally breathe.

Gash took hold of her hand. "Do you want me to back away?"

"You'd do that for me?" she asked, turning toward him. During her doubts, Gash had parked the car, and turned off the ignition.

"Don't you realize yet?"

"Realize what?"

"I'll do anything for you. Even walk away today."

She stared into his eyes, and knew without a

shadow of a doubt that he meant the words he said. "I love you," she said.

"That's all I need now, baby. I don't need anything else but those words, and you."

But in the back of his mind, she knew he'd always wonder what would have happened today.

What if Jeff does the same to another woman that he did to you?

The very thought made her cold from the inside. She didn't want anyone to suffer the way that she had suffered.

Leaning in close, she took possession of his lips. "We're going to do this, and once it's done, no more thinking about the past, just the future, right?"

"Right."

"Let's go."

They both climbed out of the car, and she took a breath as she gazed around the parking lot. Top of the range cars filled a couple of spaces, but for the most part, it was vacant.

Gash popped the trunk of the car and pulled out a bag.

"Do you want me to hold anything?" she asked.

"No, I've got it all."

"Are you sure?"

She was so damn nervous.

Gash took hold of her hand. "We're good."

With their hands locked together, they walked toward the elevator. Her heart was pounding as they started to travel toward the top floor.

We can do this.

She closed her eyes, and once again she was transported back to that hospital room, and staring at Jeff's smug face. He thought he could get away with everything. Murder wouldn't touch him, no one would touch him. She fucking hated that bastard, and Rebecca.

Her life had turned to fucking shit.

Gripping his hand a little tighter, she was more determined than ever before.

The elevator doors opened, and she walked beside Gash, her steps sure.

They got to the room number, and they both paused as nailed to the door was a single white envelope with the names Gash and Charlotte, in fancy writing.

With Gash's arms full, Charlotte grabbed the envelope opening it. Inside was a folded piece of paper and a key.

Taking out the paper, she unfolded it.

"Come in. That's all it says." She took out the key and held it up to Gash. "This doesn't feel right."

"I know. Get behind me." Gash removed his bag, opened it up, and she saw several guns, and something rolled up, which looked like some medical tools. She wasn't even going to think about that.

He checked the gun for bullets, and she guessed he got it ready for firing. She wasn't any kind of expert on guns.

"Grab the bag, and stay behind me." He took the key, sliding it into the lock.

Her stomach twisted as the door opened. Gash entered the room, and hauling the bag on her shoulder, she followed him.

Once there was enough room, she closed the door, using her foot to kick it shut.

Following behind Gash, she made sure there were several steps between them.

"Holy shit," Gash said, stopping.

"What is it?" she asked, moving to look past his shoulder.

Charlotte wished she hadn't. On the dining room

table lay a woman. She had been nailed with her arms either side of her hand. The woman's legs were spread, and she was naked. Her feet also had nails, keeping her attached to the table.

She knew without a doubt that it was Rebecca. The single birthmark on the ankle was one sign, as was the original passport that had been stabbed into her forehead. It was a brutal, violent, and bloody kill.

Unable to help it, Charlotte dropped the bag, and threw up the breakfast that she had eaten that morning.

"Not a good sight, is it?"

That voice had haunted her for seven years.

Wiping the back of her mouth, Charlotte turned toward the noise. She'd not even noticed it as she came in. Against the fake fireplace, Jeff was bound to a chair. He didn't look much better than Rebecca, but he was alive.

Gash took hold of her hand, forcing her to get behind him. "Who's here?"

Jeff laughed. "He's long gone now. Came in as if we were old pals. I should have known the truth. He had a bottle of scotch, and was talking about another job he might have for us. The bastard hadn't been here in seven years, and I should have known something was wrong." Jeff gritted his teeth and tried to fight the restraints. "He fucking drugged us." He started to shout now, and Charlotte cringed as he kept on fighting and yelling. "He made me watch what he did to her, and all the time, he was laughing. Told me that I was going to be next, but he was going to leave me to someone from my past. He kept her alive for most of it. She was screaming, begging for me to help, and I couldn't do shit."

Charlotte stared at the mess that was once Rebecca, and she felt sick to her stomach again. Rebecca didn't have a nice ending but a hard one, one that was fucking disgusting.

"Who did you work for?" Gash asked, moving toward him.

Jeff smiled. "You really think that's going to work? I'm dead either way."

Charlotte forced herself to move and looked behind Jeff. The chair he was sitting on was wired up, and she saw a countdown. "He's going to blow up," she said.

Gash looked toward her, then Jeff.

"Master and Sir do have a way to make a point, don't they?"

"Master and Sir?"

"Yep. There's no point keeping it a secret, especially as he left you a note." Jeff nodded toward the coffee table in the sitting room. Charlotte moved carefully across the apartment floor, and picked up the single envelope.

"It's addressed to you," she said, looking at Gash. She waited until Gash was beside her before she glanced over at Jeff. "The countdown on the, erm, the bomb, gave him twenty more minutes."

"You don't need to whisper. I know I'm a dead man. I'm just surprised you're not beating the shit out of me, Charlotte. After all, I did take your kid, and put you in a hospital." Jeff laughed. "You should have seen her go crazy. It took a lot of surgery to repair the damage you did to my face."

"What the fuck did you say?" Gash asked.

Charlotte saw through Jeff's act. He was terrified.

"She was knocked up with your kid, and taking it out of her was a damn pleasure. I was ordered to do it, which I thought was harsh, but it was fucking awesome."

"Who ordered you to do it?"

"Master again."

She listened to Gash and Jeff talk. All the time, she looked around the apartment, wondering what the hell was going on.

"Who is Master?" Charlotte asked.

Gash gritted his teeth.

Jeff laughed. "No one fucking knows who he is. He's a mythical being."

"What is going on?"

"Tell her, Gash."

"You don't fucking talk to her," Gash said.

"I'm dead anyway. It doesn't matter."

"He wants you to kill him," Charlotte said. "I guess getting your throat slit is much better than being blown to bits, right?"

Jeff growled, disgust clear on his face.

"Why Gash? Why him?" Charlotte asked. She looked at Jeff as he stared at her. "Why me?" This was one big vendetta against Gash, and she hadn't seen it before that moment. She looked toward Gash. "Do you know who Master is?"

"I've not got a clue," Gash said. "He's a ghost. No one knows who he is, or what he does. He's not known."

"Do you know him?"

Jeff snorted. "No one knows him. Master makes sure you know what he wants you to know, and you do what he tells you to do."

"What happened seven years ago?"

He shook his head, and Charlotte folded her arms. "Why not tell us? You're going to die anyway."

"Look, all I know is that there was a letter with five grand cash, a list of instructions and a promise of more. I did what was said in the instructions, more money was presented to me."

"Where does Rebecca come in?"

"She was given the same deal. Cash for jobs, and we met up, hit it off, and we decided to share the bounty that this job would take in. The object was to take down Gash, the member of The Skulls. No reason was given, just instructions on what to do, when to do it, and that he had to remain alive."

"What about me?"

"You weren't part of the plan until you were discovered to be pregnant. My boss didn't believe you'd be any real threat. You were fat, and Gash wasn't known for liking fat women. You were not expected, so you had to be taken care of. Also, *he* thought it would be fun to see what happened between you and Gash when he discovered the truth."

"And my unborn child?"

"We were there. We saw you touch your stomach and say Gash's name. Once you were out of it with the drugs, we got in touch with Master, and he told us the baby had to go regardless of who it was. Master wanted you out of the way but not dead."

She felt sick to her stomach. Moving behind Jeff again, she saw that they only had ten minutes. "We've got to go."

Gash didn't look happy. She walked up toward him, and grabbed his arm. "We've got to go. Once this blows, they're going to lock it all down."

She moved toward the door.

Gash stared at Jeff.

"You're not going to find him. Master only comes out when he's ready," Jeff said.

"Gash, leave it!"

She opened the door, and waited.

Finally after seconds passed, Gash rushed toward her. He took the weapons bag from her hand, and they rushed toward the elevator.

"It's going to take too long. We've got to take the stairs." Gash grabbed her hand, and shoved the door open. She rushed down behind him, following him down the flight of stairs. She was unfit, and not ready for suddenly running, but she kept on running.

Minutes passed, and they ducked as the explosion shook the building. They were two floors from the parking lot. They picked up their speed, and rushed toward their car. Gash didn't take his time to load the guns in the trunk. Jumping in the passenger seat, she waited for Gash to start the car up, and they were driving out of the parking lot. Charlotte looked back in time to see police cars arriving.

"What the fuck was that?" she asked.

"Well, it wasn't what I expected. Fuck!" Gash slammed his palm against the steering wheel. "I didn't expect Jeff to be taken out, and I didn't expect his boss to be Master."

"Who is Master?" Charlotte asked.

"He's a bad guy. From what we knew of him he dealt with women, selling girls, and using them. He brands them like cattle."

"What's his problem with you?"

"I don't have fucking clue, but I'm going to find out."

Chapter Twelve

Gash stared at the television as the news reporter talked about the explosion at the hotel. The white envelope he'd taken from the room lay on the table in church. His brothers were around them, and he rubbed his hands together, waiting for Whizz to turn off the television.

Silence fell around the room as the television went silent.

"I didn't put any explosives in the bag," Whizz said.

"Master got to Jeff before I could. Rebecca was there as well, and he'd tortured and killed her."

"Wait, Master?" Lash asked, looking toward Tiny.

The room was full with all The Skulls, and Gash nodded. "Yes, Jeff said he was hired seven years ago by someone known as Master. He never fucking met the bastard, but he was paid by him to do this kind of shit."

"Do you know Master?" Tiny asked.

"I don't know shit." Gash stood and started pacing the room. "You don't think I had a freak out when his name was mentioned? Fuck!"

"It looks like we've found our next problem," Baker said. He was sitting near the door. Out of all of The Skulls, he was the silent, brooding kind. "Master doesn't just have a problem with Chaos Bleeds, he's got a problem with us as well."

"I don't know who he is."

"Whoever it is got the means to put you in prison on bogus charges. He gives money, and we know he likes women. You need to call Devil," Tiny said, looking toward Lash.

"Did you locate Andrew?" Gash asked.

Whizz shook his head. "Nope."

"You don't think the two could be related?" Tiny asked.

"Andrew was a weak little shit. He was sick in the head, and he was all over drugs. There's no way he could be as powerful as Master," Gash said. "You've got more of a chance of Andrew selling shit about The Skulls to this mystery guy than you have of him being an actual problem."

Gash wouldn't even give his brother a thought.

"What does the letter say?" Lash asked.

"I've not opened it. I called ahead to get you guys here, and Charlotte didn't even open it." Gash reached out, opening the letter.

"What does it say?" Hardy asked.

Gash read the letter out. "Consider this a gift. I've dealt with the whore. She had to learn her place. Enjoy Jeff. He's no longer useful to me. Chat soon. M." Gash threw the letter down. "This guy is not playing by any rules."

"That's the point. There are no rules to him. He even kills people who work for him," Lash said. "This is serious. Until we know more, I want us all on lockdown. Everyone back at the club. The bitches will go back to their rooms in the basement. Kids are going to be here when they're not at school. None of the old ladies are to leave the clubhouse unless they have a prospect or one of the men with them, understood?" Lash looked at all of them.

All of the men agreed.

"Whizz, get your ass on the computer. Find everything associated with Jeff, before today, and even before Gash was sent to prison. I want to know everything about this bastard, where he went to school, his parents, even when he took a shit. The same goes for Rebecca. I want any possible lead that will show who Master is."

"I'll put a call through to speak to Brianna and Jessica. Both women were captured by Master. I might get some details, maybe even work out some facial recognition or some shit," Whizz said.

"Do that. I want us all watching our backs and the club." Lash slammed his hand down on the table. "Dismissed."

Gash left the church room before anyone else, and went to Charlotte. He tugged her in his arms and slammed his lips against hers. The guys at the club whistled and hollered, and he didn't give a fuck. Cupping her cheek, he sank his fingers into her hair, holding her close. She opened up, and he slid his tongue into her mouth, tasting her. Charlotte was his compensation for dealing with this Master shit.

Finally, she pulled away, her eyes closed. He watched her lick her lips, and his cock thickened, imagining her lips around his dick.

When she opened her eyes, she glanced around the room. "Everyone is watching us."

"I don't care." Taking hold of her hand, he turned to the guys, lifting their hands for everyone to see. "Charlotte, she's my old lady, my woman. I'll be putting a ring on her finger soon enough."

"Gash?" She tried to push their hands down, but he wasn't having that.

"No need to be embarrassed."

For the next five minutes they were surrounded by the club who congratulated them. Angel rushed toward them, pulling Charlotte in for a hug. "It's so good to see you happy."

He held Charlotte against him as Angel hugged

them. After he accepted the club's support, he bent down, pushing his shoulder against Charlotte's stomach. She let out a little squeal as he started to carry her up toward his room.

"Put me down. I can walk." She hit his ass, and he slapped hers for good measure.

She screamed again. "You did not just slap my ass."

He slapped it again. "I'm not afraid to give you what you need, baby." Another slap, and she sank her teeth into the denim of his jeans, which protected him from her bite. Gash chuckled, providing her with another slap.

Opening his bedroom door, he kicked it closed, and dropped Charlotte to the bed. He made sure her teeth were no longer sunk into his ass cheek. Capturing her hands, he pressed them beside her head.

"Are you sure about this?" she asked.

"What?"

"You just made a commitment with me in front of the entire club. Doesn't that bother you?" she asked.

"I should have made that commitment seven years ago. I'm the asshole that waited, fucking Rebecca rather than taking you. I wanted you, and if I'd acted on my feelings, this might not have happened." Dropping down, he took possession of her lips, and sighed. "Do you forgive me?" he asked.

"I've told you, Gash. There's nothing to forgive you for."

"There is. I love you, Charlotte, and I wasn't there for you."

"Don't. It's over now, and you didn't know. Jeff and Rebecca are gone. You didn't get your revenge though. Can you handle that?"

"I've got no fucking choice. It's just part of the

long list of what Master has taken from me. It's like he knows what I'll do next, always one step ahead. Jeff and Rebecca, they had it easy. He gave them an easy death."

"How? They died brutally."

Gash laughed. "You think that was brutal? Whizz had given me some surgical tools, Charlotte. I was going to tear them apart, piece by piece, and make sure they were alive while I did it. I planned to spend a great deal of time hurting them, making them beg for death long before I gave it. Master took that away, and he made sure they had it easy." The darkness inside him hadn't been appeased. Years spent in prison, he'd dreamed of the moment when he'd torture Jeff, and then Rebecca. His first plan had been to kill them both. Charlotte, she'd only been part of the plan since he first met her. All of his planning had gone to waste.

"We'll find him together. We're together, and whoever Master is, we'll deal with him like we should have done back then, together, as one." She wrapped her legs around his waist, and he ground his dick against her, loving the feel of her.

"Together." He took possession of her lips, letting go of her hands to grip her shirt. Gash stood and tore her shirt off. Charlotte got to her feet, and he tugged his own shirt off his body.

Gash watched as she stripped out of her clothes, and his mouth watered for a taste of her body, all of her. He had plenty of condoms in the drawer beside his bed, and he intended to use all of them tonight.

Removing his jeans, he stood in front of her naked, wrapping his fingers around his dick. He rubbed his cock, sliding his thumb across the tip, and rubbing the pre-cum into his flesh.

"Do you see what you do to me?" he asked.

She crossed her arms over her chest, and he

wasn't going to have that. Stepping closer to her, he took hold of her arms, and forced them away from her body.

"Never hide your body from me, baby."

"Gash?"

"Don't doubt us." He took her hand, and wrapped it around his dick. "Feel that? That's what you do to me, and there's no other woman in the world who can compete with you." Leaving her hand wrapped around his dick, he cupped her cheeks, and tilted her head back. "This is real."

"We're moving fast."

"I've never stopped wanting you, babe."

"You don't think everything is going a little crazy?"

Gash side. "Life is crazy. It's a rollercoaster ride, and we've got to ride that wave or be swallowed whole by it."

"You're not afraid of what is going on? There's a guy who set out to hurt you, and you're not caring about it?"

Pressing his head against hers, he released a sigh. "I don't have time to worry about it. Over the years I've had a lot of men who've wanted to kill me. I'm not going to stop living my life over every single person who tries to kill me." Kissing her lips, he sucked her bottom lip into his mouth, nibbling on it. "I'm going to do everything to protect you."

"I know."

"Trust me."

"I do. I just can't get it out of my head."

"Then focus on me, and I'll make sure you don't remember it, okay, baby?" he asked.

"I will."

Moving her backward, he pushed her down to the bed, following her down. "I'm going to make you forget, and you're going to love everything I do to your body." He pressed a kiss to her neck and inhaled her scent. Flicking his tongue against her pulse, he slid down her body, taking her nipple into his mouth.

He nipped at her bud before gliding across her tits to suck on her other breast. Gash loved her big tits, and he was addicted to them. Moving down, he slid his tongue down between her thighs. Opening her pussy, he flicked his tongue across her clit, and she screamed, arching up against him.

"Yes, that feels so good," she said.

"I'm only just getting started." Pushing two fingers inside her creamy cunt, he spread them open, and continued to stroke inside her, in and out.

Charlotte moaned, thrusting up against his hands.

"I want you to come for me, baby, and scream my name."

Flicking her clit, he repeated the action over and over again, working her harder. He added a third finger into her pussy, and sucked her nub into his mouth, sawing it with his teeth.

"Yes, Gash, yes."

"That's right, come for me."

He wanted her nice and soaking wet before he fucked her. Seconds later she screamed his name as she came, pushing herself down onto his fingers.

"So good." She yelled the words, and they echoed around the room.

Gash didn't give her the chance to get over her orgasm before he was sliding inside her. He'd quickly placed a condom over his dick, even as his hands were shaking. This was different. The demons from their past were gone, and they only had each other.

Slamming the last few inches inside her, he stared into her eyes, filling her body with his dick. "Do you feel me?"

"Yes."

"This is how it's always going to be between us. You belong to me, and you were always supposed to be mine."

Tears filled her eyes.

"Don't cry."

"You're saying the most beautiful things when you're supposed to be fucking me," she said.

"I'm making up for lost time." He turned them suddenly, and had her straddling him. Capturing her hips, he showed her exactly what he wanted. Charlotte gripped his shoulders and slowly started to ease up and down his dick.

Moving his hands up her body, he cupped her tits, running his thumbs across the hardened tips. "Look at you, baby, you look so fucking perfect."

He slammed up inside her as she thrust down onto his cock.

"Yes, fuck, yes," he said. "Ride me, beautiful, take what you want."

She rode up and down his cock, and he watched her, loving every single second of having his woman in his arms.

He turned her over, and started to thrust his cock deep into her, going harder still.

"Gash," she said, screaming his name.

"I know, baby, this is how it's always going to be." He rode her harder than before, wanting to brand her pussy so that it would only ever want his cock. It was sick and insane considering how many other women he'd been with, but Charlotte was all his, and he wasn't going to give her up, not ever. Charlotte belonged to him and no one else.

Pulling out of her, he started to thrust inside her.

She gripped him tightly, and he wrapped his arms around her, holding her close. Gripping her ass, he claimed her lips, slowing his pace so that he was making love to her, stretching her pussy wider with his cock.

She cried out, moaned his name, and thrust her hips up to meet him.

"Do you feel that, Char?" he asked. "I'm deep inside you, and your pussy knows what it wants, what it needs."

"I need you, Gash."

"Yes, baby, fuck. I love you." He didn't need to hear the words from her lips. He knew what her body was trying to say, and what she wouldn't let it say.

Gash would love her for the rest of his life. She consumed his thoughts, tore him apart, and made him whole again. This was the woman he'd really been in love with the whole time. Seeing her again, being around her had made him see what he wanted out of life. He wanted a change to be with her, to love her, to show her what being his woman really meant. She helped him to breathe again.

Reaching between them, he stroked her clit as he fucked her pussy, riding her hard and deep.

With a few strokes she came apart in his arms, and her pussy clamped around him. Gash gave himself over to the pleasure, finding his peak, and hurtling over it as he filled the condom with his cum.

This was his world now, Charlotte was his everything, and he intended to keep it that way.

****

Charlotte rubbed at her eyes to see sunlight streaming through the bedroom window. Gash held her tightly to him with one arm beneath her head, and the other cupping her breast. Glancing up, she saw he was indeed still asleep. She had kept him busy into the early hours of the morning, both of them making up for lost time. When she had finally fallen asleep, she'd dreamt of Rebecca and Jeff. Those two had died in a way that terrified her. Someone was after Gash, and she couldn't shake the feeling that it was going to come and bite them all in the ass.

Staring into his face, she slowly traced the curve of his cheek.

"I love you," she said. It was easier to say the words when he couldn't actually hear them. She had loved him from the first moment she saw him. Was she wrong to love him? Why shouldn't she just give into her feelings? They both wanted each other, and when he told her that he loved her, she believed him.

Sliding out from beneath him, she stared down at her nakedness, and quickly grabbed his shirt and shorts. Pushing her feet into socks, she tucked some hair behind her ear, and went in search of a bathroom.

"Who are you?"

She turned to see a brown haired woman coming out of a room, carrying a small baby in her arms.

"Erm, I'm Charlotte."

"Oh, okay, that's fine. I'm Tate, Murphy's old lady, and Tiny's daughter."

She gave a little wave. "I was looking for a toilet. I wasn't sneaking."

"No problem at all. I can show you where a bathroom is. Come on."

She followed Tate down a long hall toward a bathroom.

"There's one. I'll stand here. If you look in the little basket underneath the sink you'll find some wrapped toothbrushes. There's always a supply. They're like condoms."

"Okay," she said, speaking up loud enough so the

woman could hear.

Charlotte washed her hands after using the toilet, before hunting for a toothbrush. Once she had brushed her teeth, she opened the door to find that Tate was still there.

Before she could speak, her stomach started to growl, letting anyone who was close know that she was in fact hungry.

"Come on, Angel's probably already up. She's got a weird internal clock that makes it easy for her to wake really early. I've even known her to bake bread in the morning."

Smiling, Charlotte waited for her to lead the way.

"You're not very talkative, are you?" Tate asked.

"Erm, I don't really know what to say." She pushed her hair off her shoulder, walking side by side with the woman.

"You don't need to find something to talk about. Just be yourself, and we'll be good. I'm really easy to get along with."

"She's lying," another woman said, coming out of a room carrying a large packet of breakfast sausage.

"Fuck off, Prue."

"You're Charlotte?" Prue asked.

"Yeah, I am."

"Has Tate tried to kill you yet?"

Charlotte looked at the woman with the young baby. Tate could kill someone?

"No."

"Don't worry. Tate won't actually kill you. She just has an attitude," Prue said.

"Don't listen to her. She's just in a mood because she ended up with Zero." Tate stuck her tongue out and made gagging sounds.

Prue rolled her eyes, and all the time they kept on

moving toward the kitchen. Angel stood in the kitchen, and the scent of bread filled the large room.

"I got the sausage," Prue said. "I found Tate and Charlotte on the way back."

Angel turned, smiling at both of them, before rushing toward them, hugging them.

"I'm going to feed my kid," Tate said, taking a seat at the table.

Charlotte turned away as Tate started to nurse her child.

Another feminine sigh made her look toward the door. Eva, Tiny's old lady, came into the kitchen with Tabitha and Miles walking behind her. Charlotte did remember some of the women's and kids' names as Gash had shown her several pictures he owned.

"Angel, how do you do it?" Eva said, collapsing down at the table.

"It's not my fault. This time, this little person decided to wake me up." Angel was heavily pregnant, and from the beautiful smile on her face, she was already in love. Charlotte looked away, knowing what it was like to have those feelings of love, and wishing it was the start of something more.

One day maybe she would know that feeling again, but not right now.

"You're all lovey-dovey," Tate said.

"Does anyone know what happened with Lacey, Whizz, and Daisy?" Eva asked.

"Lash made sure the parents signed over on the adoption. Everything is going through," Angel said.

Lacey chose that moment to walk into the kitchen. Her hair was bound on top of her head, and she wore a white tank and shorts. Ink showed down her arms, as she was heavily tattooed. "What's going on?" Lacey asked. "Are we having a women's meeting?"

"Nah, talking about you and your new kid," Tate said.

A squeal released from Lacey. "We have already gone shopping. Sally and I are going to decorate her room all pink, and I've already got Whizz ordering furniture. Once all this crap blows over, I've got plans." Lacey clapped her hands, and Charlotte chuckled. The woman's excitement was rubbing off on her.

"I'm glad," Angel said.

"Tell me about it, those fuckers weren't fit to be parents," Tate said.

"Did you know they left her at school?" Eva asked.

"Yeah, Angel told me, fucking bad news."

"You get used to it," a dark skinned woman said, walking into the kitchen. "I'm Sunshine. I belong to Alex. He's the least popular of all The Skulls." Sunshine shrugged.

"We all love Uncle Alex," Tate said.

"Anyway, I just wanted you to know that you get used to the whole chaos that is the club. The women, they're all over, and it just jumps from one to the other." Sunshine chuckled.

"I hope so." Right now Charlotte didn't have a clue how she was going to get along with all of these women. They had their own little spots, their own little roles to play. She sat at the table and simply observed them. More women and then men entered. The kids ran in as well, and the whole scene before her was that of a family.

"Hey, baby," Lash said, moving behind Angel, and touching her stomach. Charlotte watched as he kissed her neck, and Angel went a dark shade of red. "Missed you this morning."

"Our baby wanted me to bake bread."

"Remember, relax, and don't exhaust yourself."

"I won't."

The scene touched her heart. This was a family, one big happy family.

"Charlotte!" Her name being hollered had everyone turning to her. Frowning, she got to her feet, and left the kitchen in time to see Gash running downstairs. He wore a pair of jeans that were unbuttoned, no shirt, and his boots weren't even tied up.

"What?" she asked, gently.

He walked toward her, taking hold of her face, and pushing her against the nearest wall. When it came to her, he seemed to have a thing about walls and pushing her up against them.

"I thought you had left."

"Why would I do that?"

"She needed the toilet," Tate said.

Charlotte's cheeks heated.

"I woke up and you were gone."

"Together forever, right? We're in this together."

He nodded, and before she could say anything else, he slammed his lips down on hers, claiming a kiss she hadn't been ready for. His lips were hard and demanding. She had no choice but to open up, and take the kiss that he gave. He slid his tongue into her mouth, and she met his strokes, remembering how good he felt licking her pussy.

Pressing her thighs together, she moaned, wrapping her arms around his neck, holding him again.

"Ew, Uncle Gash is being so gross," Tabitha said, rushing past them.

Gash pulled away, and she saw a large, older looking man chuckle. "She thinks she wants to marry Simon."

"I guess you've got nothing to worry about with

her then, eh, Tiny?" Gash said.

Tiny burst out laughing. "If I could, I'd stop all of my kids from growing up. I don't want them to."

The large man she now knew as Tiny walked into the kitchen.

"Simon?" Charlotte asked.

Gash pointed into the room at a young girl with brown hair. "See that little girl?" She nodded. "Well, she's got a thing going with the son of another gang. You see why Tiny was laughing? She can't handle us kissing, so she's not going to want to kiss Simon, Devil's son."

Once again she was frowning. "That girl doesn't look a day older than six. Tiny does realize she's going to grow up, her body is going to develop, and she's going to want to do more than kiss?"

Gash laughed. "Do me a favor, if you want to live long in this club, don't tell Tiny that. We're all keeping that knowledge from him."

Charlotte chuckled. "Really?"

"Yes."

"I think I'll enjoy being part of this club?"

"Only think? Babe, this is more than a club."

"I know. You're a family, and I'm starting to see that now."

Gash kissed her deeply, and she moaned. His rock hard cock dug against her hip. Her stomach started to growl, letting everyone close to her know that she was indeed hungry.

"Damn, you're hungry."

"That's why I came downstairs in the first place."

"We better get some food inside you." He took hold of her hand, pushing the way into the kitchen, which was now crowded. She saw a couple of tables were set up in the bar area of the club with men eating.

"Angel, woman, I want food for my old lady, and

she needs it now."

"Gash, stop it," Charlotte said.

"I'm cooking as fast as I can. Do you like biscuits, Charlotte?" Angel asked.

"Yes."

Within minutes she was sitting on Gash's lap at the table with a plate of sausages, biscuits, and gravy. She didn't know how she was going to eat it all, but she was going to give it a go.

Gash reached around her with a fork, and started to help her eat the food. She liked the intimacy of their eating, and knew it was something she was looking forward to for many years to come.

****

Sandy stared across the clubhouse as Stink fixed up his bike. The club was all on lockdown once again, and she was strangely happy about that. She shared his room, and throughout the night Stink would hold her tightly against him. The best part of her night was being in Stink's arms. He made her feel safe and happy.

"What are you staring at or do I already know?" Rose asked.

"Nothing."

"You can't fool me. You've got your eye on that hunky man there with no ability to smell. He's a hot choice, and everyone knows he's crazy about you."

"Stop it?" Sandy asked, hating how guilty she felt.

"Why? Can't stand to see what is in front of you? He loves you, Sandy."

"I was a club whore."

"So? Are you saying women who fuck any man can't find love or be happy? That seems a bit … mean."

Sandy sighed. "No, I'm not saying that."

"Stink's not married."

"I know that."

"Then what is stopping you?"

"He deserves someone better than me. He's a good guy, and I'm not that girl."

"Good, because he's not looking for a girl. He's looking for a woman, and he's looking at you. You're the one he wants. Stop being an insecure bitch, and go and get him. He loves you, and life is just so damn hard, don't make it harder."

Rose tapped her shoulder, and Sandy sighed.

What would be wrong with actually giving in, and finding out what this attraction was like? Stink wasn't a bad guy.

Making up her mind, she made her way toward him. Even though it was cold outside, Stink was still working on his bike. He loved his bike.

"What's going on, Sandy?" he asked before she even spoke.

"How did you know it was me?"

"I know you, babe." He stood, wiping his hand on an already streaked dirty cloth.

"It's not exactly attractive calling someone predictable."

"Didn't call you predictable. I wouldn't dream of labeling you with that kind of shit."

He stared at her, and like so many times before, her heart started to pound. What was it about this man that had her melting from the inside out? They hadn't done anything but share a few fleeting kisses. Yes, she shared his bed, but it hadn't actually led to anything.

"What have you come to talk to me about?" Stink asked.

"I want to give us a try."

She ran fingers through her hair, suddenly nervous.

He dropped the cloth to the floor and stepped up toward her. The scent of leather and oil surrounded him. "It's about time you came to your senses." He sank his fingers into her hair, and slammed his lips down on hers. There was no more fight within her, especially as she wanted him as much as he wanted her.

Chapter Thirteen

"What about Millie?" Baker asked.

He looked at Lash, Nash, Alex, and Tiny. They were looking through some paperwork that Whizz had left with them before going back up to his room.

"What about her?" Lash asked.

"I want to bring her to the club for protection." Baker twisted his hands, hating the nerves that were rushing through his body. He'd never been this fucking nervous before in his life, and it was pissing him the fuck off. Millie was just another woman, but he couldn't bring himself to think of her as just another woman. She was a sweet woman, so sweet that she didn't even think about her own damn safety, and it was driving him crazy. The club was on lockdown, and he wanted his woman, not that Millie knew she belonged to him. It was a technicality that he intended to rectify at some point. Only, he'd not done it yet.

"Seriously, dude, you claimed her as your woman, go and get her," Nash said.

Heat filled his cheeks. "She, erm, she doesn't know."

All of the men turned to look at him.

"Okay, let me get this straight. You've been dating a woman, and she doesn't have a clue that you're actually dating. We've been keeping an eye on her shop."

"It hasn't ever come up," Baker said.

"For fuck's sake, Baker, man up and grow some fucking balls," Lash said.

Anger hit Baker hard. The men turned to Lash in surprise.

"What? You want me to pussyfoot around him? He's got a woman out there, and it's not up to us to make him make a decision. He either wants Millie or he doesn't. She's a nice woman, and Angel likes her, okay? If Baker hurts her, it's going to hurt Angel, and if you hurt Angel because you hurt her friend, I'll fucking hurt you, do you get me?"

"I get you."

Turning away, he made his way outside. Stink and Sandy were wrapped around each other, and he just didn't want to see that shit.

It's time to move on.

He was once married to the most beautiful woman he'd ever seen, until Millie. Happily married, baking every single day, and now, he was running with The Skulls.

You were always more than a baker.

Pushing the thoughts out of his mind, he rode into town toward Millie's toy shop. She ran the only toy shop in Fort Wills.

Baker loved being around her. She was so damn sweet, even more so than Angel. Millie was also oblivious to the dangers in the world. Once he was outside her shop, he climbed off his bike and made his way inside. He paused as he took in the sight of her. She was sitting on a stool behind the counter, a pencil running across her lip as she tried to do the crossword puzzle. Her hair was pulled into a ponytail.

Clearing his throat, he waited as she looked up. The moment she saw him, she smiled.

"Baker, I wasn't expecting you." She placed the puzzle down, and climbed off her chair, rounding the counter.

She wore a pair of pale blue jeans and a long shirt. None of her curves were on display even though he knew that she possessed them.

"I want you to come to the clubhouse," he said.

"Why?" She frowned, and Lash's words ran through his head. He had to have balls, and right now, he wanted Millie at the clubhouse.

"Look, you're my woman, and I'm not going to pretend that you're not." He moved past her, grabbing her bag and keys, shutting down the computer as he talked. "The club is on lockdown, and I want you there."

"Baker, you're scaring me. I don't understand."

He stepped up close to her, placing her jacket over her shoulders. "You're mine. You'll always be mine, and I'm not going to pretend anymore."

"We've had a couple of dates. I don't understand."

Grabbing her arms, he pulled her against him, slamming his lips against hers. Sinking his fingers into her hair, he moaned as her sweet scent surrounded him. He'd never known heaven like this, and he never wanted to know anything else.

Suddenly, Millie pushed him hard.

"No, you don't just get to kiss me and think everything is going to be okay."

"I claimed you as mine, and that puts you at risk."

"I'm not going with you."

Baker sighed, pulling out his cell phone. He dialed the club, and waited. Ink was the first brother to answer.

"I need a car."

"You took your bike."

"Yeah, Millie is being difficult."

Millie rolled her eyes and moved back toward the counter. She grabbed her bag from him, and continued to glare.

"Damn, I'll be there."

Closing his cell phone, he stared at Millie. His cock was so damn hard. He didn't know why, but he had always assumed that she'd be happy to be on his radar when in fact, she couldn't stand to be near him.

She folded her arms and looked at everything but at him.

"You can't seriously tell me that you didn't know this was coming?" he asked.

"I thought you wanted to be my friend."

"I took you on dates."

"So? You talked about going out as friends. This, between us, it hasn't been happening." She shook her head. "This isn't fair."

"Everyone knows I want you but you," he said.

"You're still mourning the death of your wife and unborn child, Baker. You don't want me. You see me as easy."

"I don't see me fucking you right now."

She snorted. The sound was totally unladylike, and he'd never thought he'd hear her make the sound. "What is it? Chubby Millie wouldn't be able to turn down a chance at a hot guy like you. You just assumed I wanted you."

Baker growled. "Don't say shit like that."

"What? The truth? Come on, you had to admit you didn't even for a second doubt that I would want you."

He couldn't deny it. Baker hadn't once thought that she would turn him down.

"You don't want me?"

"No. I don't want a man that is so in love with his first wife that he gives up baking, and moves away to start a new life with a club. You're not over her."

It was strange. Baker expected pain at her words, but there was none. It had been several years since his wife had been killed in a hit-and-run. Staring at Millie, he forgot all about his wife, and more days would pass before he gave her a thought. He wouldn't lie, he loved his wife, but he wanted to move on.

Before he could say anything more, the sound of a car horn honking stopped him. "That's our ride." Moving around the counter, he shoved his shoulder against her stomach, and hauled her up, slapping her ass.

"Put me down!"

He slapped her ass again, finally filled with euphoria. Millie may not be ready for him, but he was more than ready for her.

"If I ever hear you say shit about yourself again, I'll spank your fucking ass."

She slapped his ass, thumbing him. "Put me down."

He grabbed her bag and left the shop. Ink was standing by the car with a door open. "I've already put the child locks on. You don't need to worry about her escaping."

Baker threw the keys at Ink. "Lock up the shop will you, and follow us back on the bike."

"You're an asshole, Baker. This is not fair."

"I claimed you," he said.

"But I don't claim you. This has to be a two way street."

"That's all right. I'm more than happy taking my time to convince you that you belong to me." Pushing her into the car, he slammed the door closed, and rushed around to the driver's side, climbing in.

"I'm so mad at you right now."

"You'll be safe, and we'll talk about other shit in time."

He pulled away from the toy shop, and glanced into the back. Millie had put her seatbelt on, and was refusing to talk to him.

I can handle that, baby, but I'm not giving you

up, not anymore.

Staring down at his wedding band, he did something he never thought he'd do. He removed the ring that bound him to another woman. It was time for him to move on.

****

Charlotte stood outside while the kids were on the playing area. They all looked happy. Tate was watching the kids with her as Lash had to take Angel to the hospital for a check up on the baby.

"Hey everyone," Kelsey said, coming toward them. She held Markus's hand and opened the gate, letting him go.

"Ah, finally, you join the real people."

"You're just freaked out that I work at a dentist."

Charlotte couldn't help but wince at the thought of going to the dentist. There was nothing thrilling about that at all. "You're a dentist?"

"I'm a dental nurse."

Scrunching up her face, Charlotte shook her head.

Kelsey laughed. "No one likes hearing about my work. You're not the only one."

"I work as a receptionist for a law firm, not exactly exciting," Charlotte said. She would have to get in touch with them. Glancing back at the clubhouse, she couldn't help but smile. There was no going back to that life with Gash. This was her life now, and she didn't have a problem about that. It was time for her to move on.

Rubbing her gloved hands together, she turned to the kids, watching them play.

Daisy was on the swing with Tabitha on the other. Anthony stood behind both girls, pushing them.

The love of the club was so palpable that she couldn't imagine being anywhere else.

"Here comes trouble," Tate said.

Charlotte had already clocked her man dressed in a leather jacket. He wrapped his arms around her, tugging her close. "It's cold."

"I know, but I wanted to watch the kids."

"Are you sad?"

"Why? Because of what we lost?" He nodded. "No. I'm not sad. I'm happy, really happy."

"That could have been us, babe," Gash said, pointing at Killer and Kelsey.

"It could have been, but there's no stopping it from being us." She placed his hands on her stomach. "When we're ready, we can try again."

"You can still have kids?"

"Yes. Nothing was ruined. When I got out of the hospital, I had all the checkups done to make sure I was fine. I am."

"Soon," he said, kissing her neck.

"Soon." She closed her eyes, leaning against him, content. He was the love of her life, and even though they'd been apart for many years, she wasn't going to stop loving him. He was her man, and she'd stick by him for the rest of her life.

"It's about time we saw you happy," Angel said.

Charlotte opened her eyes, and saw Angel waddling toward them, Lash by her side.

"Mom," Anthony said, rushing toward her. The little boy paused in front of her and wrapped his arms around his mom.

"Honey, you're going to have a baby sister," Angel said, bending down, and picking him up.

"Nope, not happening." Lash grabbed Anthony, holding his son. "You can hold our son as soon as you're not pregnant anymore."

Anthony burst out laughing.

Angel rolled her eyes. "Anyway, you look really happy," she said, looking toward them.

Charlotte smiled.

"I am happy," Gash said. "I have the woman I've always wanted."

He always knew when to say the right thing.

For the rest of the afternoon she stayed in Gash's arms as they supervised all of the kids. Several of the club brothers joined them, and she listened as they spoke to Gash before heading toward their bike.

Gash was humming in her ear, and she was getting more aroused with every passing second. His fingers stroked across her wrist, and the heat spilled from the lips of her pussy, coating her panties with her cream.

Licking her lips, she was about to suggest they go to his room when a car, followed by the sound of a bike entered the clubhouse.

"Baker, I swear, you're going to be sorry."

They both turned to watch Baker open a car door, and haul a woman out, and carry her into the clubhouse.

"Deal with it. This is how it's going to go, Millie," Baker said.

"Come on, let's go on inside."

Charlotte made sure that Kelsey and Eva had the kids before heading inside with Gash.

"You're being a brute and a Neanderthal," Millie said.

Baker had put Millie down, but he also had all the exits covered. Even Gash was standing in the doorway so she couldn't escape.

"What is going on?" Angel asked, coming out of the kitchen, wiping her hands.

"I don't like Baker," Millie said. "He's kidnapped me."

Angel placed her hands on her hips and glared at

Baker. "What are you doing?"

"She's my woman. We're on lockdown. There's a threat, and I'm not going to let anything happen to her. She's got to deal with it."

"I do not. I don't belong to you, and I'm never going to belong to you." Millie crossed her arms, looking like a scolded child.

Charlotte's heart went out to the woman. She looked so sweet, and a little put out by the whole experience.

"She doesn't leave," Baker said, and made to walk away.

"See, how can I belong to a guy who can't even finish what he started? You kidnap me, and dump me on your friends." Millie got to her feet, and pushed past him harder. "I'll be happy to help you, Angel."

"You're not going to throw a tantrum?" Baker asked.

"Not at you. You want me to stay here, fine. I'll stay with my friends, but don't ever expect me to accept an invitation to a movie with you again."

Gash chuckled. "Oh, it's going to a tough couple of weeks."

Lash was laughing as well when his cell phone started to ring. It was late evening, and Charlotte's stomach started to growl. The scents coming out of the kitchen were making her mouth water.

The smile on Lash's face dropped. "What the fuck?"

Gash tensed behind her, and the men lost all sense of humor. It was scary how quickly they all turned.

"Is he okay?" Lash asked. "Fuck, okay, I'll talk to the brothers. Take care, brother."

Lash hung up the phone.

"What is it?" Tiny and Alex asked at the same

time.

"Master struck, and Spider's in the hospital fighting for his life. Devil doesn't know if he's going to wake up."

This was bad. Charlotte knew it was bad by the way the men sobered up.

"There's more," Lash said. "Master has also taken two girls. One of them is a dancer at the club, and the other is her sister who is ill. I didn't get more out of Devil. He wanted to get back and check on his guy. I'm opening up our house. The women are coming to stay with us, and we're going to do a meet up."

"You sure we can handle that?" Nash said.

"I don't give a fuck what we can and cannot handle. It's what we're going to do. It's the right thing to do."

Gash took hold of Charlotte, tugging her into his arms. The men started moving around, and she watched as the kids and women were called inside.

"Come on, I want to talk to Whizz before we're all fighting for food."

He kept hold of her hand as they made their way up the back of the clubhouse where all of the rooms were. Gash didn't even knock. He just entered the room. Whizz was sitting at a computer, typing away.

"Why am I not surprised that you have no respect for personal space?" Whizz said.

"We're all in lockdown."

"I know, and even with all of you guys around, I've got two girls now that take Lacey's attention from me, not that I'm jealous or anything."

"Yeah, my heart is bleeding for you. What do you know?" Gash asked.

Charlotte walked into the room and leaned against the wall. The bed was rumpled, and she wasn't exactly in the mood to sit on someone else's bed, especially one that had seen a lot of action.

She stayed silent as Gash stood behind Whizz. The wall of screens was impressive but not nearly as much as the ones at his home.

"Any news?"

"Not the kind of shit you're going to like."

"Try me."

"Okay, so Master appeared about twelve years ago, or at least the rumor mill, texts, emails, alerts that people had tried to hide, but the internet isn't like your standard paperwork. There's always a trail, a long, dirty trail."

"Get to the point!"

Charlotte rubbed her hands together to try to warm herself up. Her gut was twisting as Whizz spoke. Master was sounding like a ghost that couldn't be caught.

"Master doesn't act like everyone expects him to. He's cruel, and there are times he employs minions to do his dirty work, but that's not always the case. What makes him different is the fact he likes to get his hands dirty. No one knows who he is as his name has never been mentioned before. They only know him as Master. He's unpredictable."

"And this son of a bitch has an issue with me?"

"Yes."

Gash cursed and shook his head. "You've got no idea who he is?"

"No, none. I've got clues. He's into everything when it comes to trafficking. There are no limits to what he'll sell. For himself, he only takes women, and most of them end up dead, discovered months after they were taken with a brand on their thigh."

"What the fuck is this man's deal?"

"I don't know, but I'm trying to access all the

CCTV in the area that Devil texted me. I'm going to find this fucker if it kills me. Just make sure my girls are looked after," Whizz said, cricking his neck and getting to typing again.

Chapter Fourteen

"We need to go shopping for supplies," Steven said, coming out of the pantry.

Charlotte swallowed her porridge and watched as Lash cursed. Gash rubbed the back of her neck as the tension in the club mounted.

Ever since the news that one of Chaos Bleeds crew had been taken and injured it had set all of The Skulls on edge. The kids were behaving, which was a surprise as Charlotte had heard the women speaking of them being terrors.

"Fuck! We need food. Devil will be arriving in a couple of days. He's packing his women up, but he doesn't want to risk leaving Spider. We're waiting for him to wake up, and so far, he hasn't."

"I can go," Charlotte said, speaking up. She wanted to go to the store to pick up some clothes for herself, and some supplies. It had been well over a week since she'd gone to the store for herself, and it would also give her a chance to call her boss up, and let him know she wasn't returning. In time she'd also need to empty out her apartment. Maybe she could pick up a paper so she could start looking for places for her and Gash to live.

"No," Gash said.

"What?" She turned toward him.

"You're not going."

"I want to go. There're some things I'd like to get."

"I said no."

She felt the eyes of the club focus on them. "You know, I've put up with a great deal of your shit since you came back into my life, and for the most part, I accepted it. I won't be going alone, right?" She looked around the room.

"I need to go," Sally said, speaking up.

"I'll go," Steven said.

"Me too." This came from Ink, Adam, and Twisted.

"See, I'll be more than safe." She cupped his cheek. "Please, I want to go and get some things. Let me."

Gash sighed, and after several seconds passed, he nodded. "Fine. I'll come—"

"I need you here, Gash, to look over our other supplies," Lash said.

She saw her man grit his teeth, clearly not happy with being told that he couldn't do something. He really didn't like being told no.

Charlotte laughed. "See, we're both going to be busy, and we've both got stuff to do. I'm going to pick us up a newspaper as well. We can go apartment hunting. How does that sound?"

"Fine! You keep an eye on her, do you understand me?" Gash said, pointing at the men.

"We will." They all agreed in unison.

Finishing her porridge, she took the bowl into the kitchen. She helped do some dishes, and then the guys shouted they were rounding up to leave. Kissing Gash, she followed Sally, Steven, Ink, Adam, and Twisted. Angel was asking for several items, and Charlotte made a mental note to pick them up.

Climbing into the back of the truck, she saw with Sally, who was looking out of the window. She saw that Steven kept glancing toward Sally.

"Are you okay?" Charlotte asked.

"I'm fine."

"Steven keeps glancing over here."

Sally sighed. "He thinks I've got a crush on him."

"And you don't." They spoke quietly so no one heard them.

"It's complicated," Sally said.

"Okay, I get complicated, believe me, I do." Charlotte ran fingers through her hair. "You know, I never thought I'd breathe again."

"I heard you had it rough. No one has actually talked to me about it. It's just what I've heard Mom and Dad talking about."

Charlotte showed Sally her inner wrists. "I went through a really dark period in my life when Gash was sent to prison. I lost a child, and I went a little, erm, crazy. I get complicated."

"You tried to kill yourself."

"More than once, and these are not my only scars. It'll get better."

"He's full of himself."

"But you *do* have a crush, so I guess he has a reason to be," Charlotte said. "Don't worry. Your secret is more than safe with me."

"I don't want to ruin my life," Sally said. "I'm so scared that I'm going to do or say something and they're going to get rid of me. I can't stand the thought of losing The Skulls."

Charlotte grabbed the young woman's hand and squeezed. "I have the same fears. They're a family, and you want to be part of that more than anything. I get it." She rested her head against Sally's shoulder. "They're not going to get rid of you. You're one of them."

The car pulled into the busy supermarket, and they all climbed out. She hooked her arm through Sally's and made her way into the store. When she saw the clothing section, she split from the group, and started grabbing some items that she figured she'd need.

Once she was done, she made her way back, but she needed to use the bathroom.

"I'm going to the toilet. I'll be right back." Ink made to follow her, and she shook her head. "Seriously, we're in a crowded shop. Let me take a pee in peace." Before he had a chance to say anything, she was gone, rushing toward the bathroom.

The bathroom was silent, and she rushed into a stall. The pop music played in the background after she finished her break, and she left the stall, washing her hands.

"Charlotte Bilson, we've never had the pleasure of meeting in person."

She spun around to find a large guy coming out of a stall, the stall next to hers. Her heart started to race.

"Do I know you?"

"You know of me, but you don't actually know me." He started chuckling, and she took in his business suit—it had to be designer, and expensive.

"You're Master." She frowned. He couldn't be Master. He'd been terrorizing Chaos Bleeds, not that she knew where they lived, but there was no way he could be here, could he? "No, you can't. You've just put Spider—
"

"Into the hospital, yes. You see, darling, the key to being successful and powerful is having minions willing to get dirty for you, and that's exactly what I have." He leaned against the stall as if he didn't have a care in the world.

"You didn't hurt Spider?"

"Oh, I hurt him, and I currently have two things that he considers precious in my possession. I'll give them up when I get what I want. I love to play games."

"Games?"

"Yeah, I think the funniest one I've played so far

is guess who. None of you have a clue who I am. You, I don't blame, you don't know me. Others, I'm a little disappointed, but that's okay. I'm never disappointed for long."

He struck before she could defend herself. Master grabbed her, slamming her up against the bathroom mirror, so the glass smashed. He winded her, landing a blow to her stomach, and she collapsed onto the floor.

Charlotte couldn't stop him. He picked her up by fisting his hand in her hair, and tugging so she had no choice but to get to her feet. She cried out from the pain.

"Now, let's see what Gash will do when he knows I've got you, his precious little bitch. I wonder if he'll pick to save you, or take me out, Charlotte. What do you think?"

"Let me go!"

"No." He wrapped his arm around her waist, and she felt something hard pressed against her side. "We're going to leave this store, and you're not going to stop. You try to get attention, I will shoot you, and then I will take Sally in your place. Would you like me to do that? That little bitch knows what it's like to be used and abused. I'm sure there are enough men willing to pay the price to fuck that bitch until she's torn in fucking two."

The mention of the young woman had Charlotte freezing. She couldn't let anything happen to her.

"I'll behave."

"Good. Let's go."

She shouldn't have told Ink to leave her alone. They left the bathroom, and she gritted her teeth as she saw there was a side entrance, leading away from the store. There was no chance of her escaping. He shoved her through the door, and then into a dark windowed car. Master didn't allow her to sit on a seat. He pushed her to the floor and forced her to kneel with no protection.

Tears stung her eyes, and she turned her head to the side so she could breathe.

"I like my bitches on the floor, knowing what is good for them. You give a whore an inch, they'll take a fucking mile." He wrapped her hair around his fist, pressing her head against the seat. The pain was instant, and she cried out as the tears started to fall. "You wanted to die, didn't you? For a long time, you wanted to take your own life, and give up."

"Stop," she said, whispering the words. She had never been so afraid before in her life.

"Why? I'm giving you what you want." He pressed the gun to the back of her head. "I'll give you what you failed to do yourself."

She shook her head, crying out and whimpering. "Stop."

"Do you want me to end your miserable, childless life?"

"No, please stop." She didn't want to die.

Master laughed. "That's okay. I've got another game I want to play first. Let's see how much Gash loves you."

****

Gash looked around at the weapons in the basement. They had quite the collection ready in case of a war.

"Tiny believed in being prepared, and I believe in shooting first and asking questions later," Lash said.

"We haven't got time to fuck about. Not with our families' lives at stake," Nash said, looking through the ammunition. "We're getting too old for this shit."

"We'll deal with Master."

"Any news on Spider?" Gash asked.

"None."

Gash nodded. "We'll wait." Rubbing the back of

his head, he stared around the room. "I'm going to ask Charlotte to marry me."

"Well that was fucking fast," Nash said.

"I love her. She's the only woman I've ever loved. I want to get my ring on her finger before she realizes that I'm not what she deserves."

"Angel deserves better than me. She deserves a man who has a nine to five job, who'll bring home a steady wage, and won't be at risk of dying when he goes out on the road. I thought about all of the shit kind of reasons why Angel and I shouldn't be together, and then I thought of the most important reason we are together."

"What's that?" Gash asked.

"There's no one else in this world who'll give her the kind of love I can. I worship Angel. She's the love of my life, and no one out there can make her feel as special as I can."

"That sounded romantic. Did you know your brother was romantic?" Gash asked.

"Nah, he's a pussy deep down. I bet he even writes her poems and shit."

They both started laughing, and Gash headed toward the stairs leading out of the basement to answer his ringing phone.

"Hello," he said.

"A little birdie told me that you're looking for me."

Gash frowned. "Who is this?"

"Well, I never said you were bright. First letter is M, the last is R. Do you want me to spell it out to you?" he asked.

"Master?" Gash looked around the room as people noticed he was on the phone.

"Wow, a point to you. You know how to spell."

"What the fuck do you want?"

"It's not about what I want. It's about what you want."

"What do I want?" Gash asked. Tiny moved to stand beside him.

"Tell me, Gash, have you been in love recently?" Before he had a chance to answer, he heard a scream, Charlotte's scream.

"You fucking bastard. Let her go. You let her go!"

"Oh, I'll let her go. I have to say I'm struggling here. She wanted to die, and I'm more than happy to give her what she wants. What do you think of a bullet through the head?"

Another scream, and Gash slammed his fist against the wall. "Leave her the fuck alone!" He yelled the words. His heart was pounding, and when he got his hands on this fucker, he was going to tear him apart.

"You know what, I think burning. That would be an interesting way to go, painful, and Charlotte deserves pain."

"I'm going to kill you."

"Threats are nice. They turn me on, but I'm curious how much in love you are with this woman. Come to where this all started. Come to the first place you met Charlotte."

"What?"

"If you remember that, you might have a chance to save her. I'm about to light a match, and I'm not interested in waiting. Oh, and come alone. I think it's time you and I meet."

Master hung up the phone, and Gash didn't stand around. He rushed out of the clubhouse with several of the guys on his tail.

"He has Charlotte. I can't stay around, and I've got to go alone. Get Ink and those fuckers back. I'm going to fucking kill them."

"Gash, this could be a trap," Tiny said.

"I haven't got time to think. He's going to kill Charlotte, and I can't let my woman burn."

He rode out of the clubhouse as darkness started to fall. Gash remembered where he had first met Charlotte. It had been at the old apartment building where he fucked Rebecca, where everything had been fucked from the start.

Don't die. Don't die. Don't die.

Through the whole of his life, he'd never been afraid. Not once had he ever been afraid. Going to prison, getting beat up, he had lived through hell, and yet throughout it all, he'd not been afraid, and he had accepted his fate. Right here, right now, he couldn't handle it. Charlotte's scream would be something he'd not be able to forget for a long time.

He had failed her.

Master wouldn't have gotten to her if he'd gone to the shops with her.

Fuck!

Riding toward the apartment building that had been rundown and was the filthiest building he ever seen, Gash pulled up, and climbed off his bike. He rushed toward the door, and stopped as he heard his voice. Master's voice.

"Don't you want to see who I am?" Master asked.

Gash was going to kill this fucker. He was going to destroy him, and laugh as he did.

"You messed with the wrong man," Gash said, turning around, and coming to a stop. He'd never expected to see him again, and hadn't given him a thought, as he'd assumed he was dead.

"Hello, brother."

"Andrew." He stared at the brother he'd not seen

in over fifteen years. The last time he'd seen the man before him was when Tiny told him he couldn't join the club.

"I go by Master now." The man before him was his brother, but he'd changed. There was no sign of him being an addict. The suit was expensive, and he was filled out. "Do you like?"

"What the fuck are you doing?" This was the man who had been hurting women. His own brother had paid Jeff and Rebecca to set him up for rape and murder.

"I'm playing. You know as kids we always liked to play."

"You also liked to trap and torture animals."

"I've upgraded. I torture people now, men and women. It's fun." Andrew smiled. "I like to keep women as my pets now."

"You brand them."

"You've heard of my work."

"What the fuck is your problem?" He charged toward his brother, slamming his fist against Andrew's face.

His brother laughed, wiping away some blood from the cut lip. "You sure know how to pack a punch."

Screams came from behind him, and Gash looked back. Charlotte was in there.

"I'm going to have to ask you, brother. Do you love your woman enough to let me go?" Andrew asked.

"What the fuck did you do?"

"All will be revealed. I sent Whizz an email. It has a rather poetic message."

"You're my brother," Gash said.

"I wasn't your brother a long time ago, even before we tried to join The Skulls. You should tell Tiny that it was his mistake, and he had it coming. MCs have a very short life. It's outdated, and they're all going to move on because of men like me."

"No one is going to stop The Skulls."

Master laughed. "I'm not like any other enemy you've faced, Gash."

"We've defeated every single person who has come to take us down."

"It's going to be interesting, isn't it, Gash? You won your chance at being part of The Skulls."

"You were a fucking addict, Andrew. You were more interested in getting high than you were in being loyal. The point of the club is to watch each other's back." Gash didn't even know why he was justifying himself to his brother. Andrew had always been a sick fuck, torturing animals when they were growing up, hurting people every chance he got. He should have stopped him, and now others were going to suffer.

Andrew shrugged, running his hands down his pristine suit. "Let's see who will win this time. I'd say we're equally suited. I'll give you a proper burial when it is all over."

This time Gash laughed. "You see, Andrew, the reason we're not going down is because you sent us everything you've got, and yet, we're still fighting strong. You can't defeat us. We will kill you."

There was an explosion in the distance, and he ducked as glass rained down from the building.

This time, Andrew laughed. "Go on then, kill me, Gash, but then you'll never find Spider's women, and Charlotte will die. Take me out, and you lose the time you need to save her. I guess that's not a hardship. She's nothing but a fucking whore."

The memory of Charlotte's scream echoed through his mind. Andrew took a step back. "Choose, brother, me or Charlotte. Who is it going to be? Tick tock, Charlotte or me?"

As he stared at Andrew, the man he needed to kill to stop the evil that was going on in the world, he thought about Charlotte. His memories went back to the moment he first saw her, and how attracted he was to her. Next, he remembered having fun and dancing with her late one night while he waited for Rebecca to come home. The memories went by to the point where he kissed her that morning.

He couldn't lose her.

This was the hardest decision he ever had to make. Before him was the reason his club, his family had been hurting, and it would be so easy to kill him, but Andrew would make it hard for him. He'd make it so Gash lost more time.

Either save his family from future pain, or save his woman.

Gash didn't hesitate.

He turned his back on Andrew and rushed into the burning building.

"Charlotte!" He yelled her name, rushing upstairs.

The first place they'd met was inside her room, and he ran as fast as he could to get to her. He couldn't let anything happen to her.

"Charlotte!"

He kept shouting her name, rushing upstairs, and making his way toward her. His heart raced, and as he got to her floor, the smoke started to get thicker.

"Help me, please, help me, I don't want to die."

Charlotte's words had him rushing toward her room. He slammed open the door, and there, chained to the radiator was his woman.

"Gash?"

He rushed toward her, staring down at where she was handcuffed to the radiator. Not giving himself a chance to think, he pulled on the pole.

"Come on, baby, I need you to pull with me."

Together they tugged, and when that didn't help, Gash lost his temper.

"Go, Gash," Charlotte said. "I don't want you to die. I love you. I love you so much."

He bent down, cupping her cheeks. "You're not going to tell me that you love me, and then leave me. I'm getting you out." He tore some of her shirt, and rushing toward the sink. The water was dirty, but it would give them some time. Gash placed the cloth over her nose and mouth, and did the same for him. Then he found an old wrench. Grabbing the metal bar, he pried it against the wall and the radiator. Using all of his weight, he pried and the metal snapped. Charlotte slid her hands out of the gap, and together, they started rushing out of the apartment building. Leaving the room, they entered a cloud of smoke. Grabbing the cuffs, he ran toward the stairs, and Charlotte kept up with him.

Together they charged out of the apartment building, and when they were clear, he picked Charlotte up in his arms, carrying her toward his bike. Removing the fabric from their faces, he cupped her face, and slammed his lips down on hers.

In the distance he heard the rumbling of bikes, followed by the sirens.

"I love you," Charlotte said. "I love you so much."

"I fucking love you, baby."

"You picked me. I didn't think you were going to pick me."

"I'd pick you every single time. You're my woman, and I fucking love you."

He stroked the bruise on her cheek.

"You let him get away."

"I couldn't live without you. Andrew, he's not going anywhere."

"Andrew? But—"

"Master is my brother."

"Gash."

He shook his head. "Don't worry about it. I'll take him out soon enough."

When his brothers came to a stop in front of him, Gash looked at Tiny. "It's Andrew. Master is Andrew."

"We need to get out of here," Tiny said.

Lash tossed him a set of keys. "We always have spares."

He unlocked Charlotte's handcuffs, and climbed on the back of his bike, waiting for his woman to straddle behind him. Staring at the apartment building, Gash wondered about what was to come. His brother was unpredictable, and he'd never for a second believed it would be Andrew who was Master, their enemy.

Gash would watch his back because Andrew didn't know it yet, but by revealing his identity, he had just brought about his downfall.

Andrew was unpredictable as Master. None of The Skulls and Chaos Bleeds knew what to expect of Master. Knowing it was Andrew, Gash knew his brother. He'd watched him growing up, and now, Gash knew exactly how to play that fucker's game.

He could have had him tonight, but he'd have lost Charlotte.

With Charlotte by his side, he'd be able to take Andrew down.

****

"You're an idiot," Sir said.

Andrew rolled his eyes. He'd picked Russell up along the way over fifteen years together. Russell had nothing to do with The Skulls or Chaos Bleeds, and that was what Andrew wanted. Russell could go through towns undetected, unlike him.

"Be careful," he said.

"You showed yourself."

"What fun is it taking down one's brother, if he doesn't know it? For ten years I've sent many people to take out The Skulls and Chaos Bleeds, and yet, all have failed. I'm not going to fail. Remember the old adage, you want a job done right, you've got to do it yourself."

"Is that why you took out Rebecca and Jeff?"

"No. Rebecca and Jeff had turned against me, Russell. They had evidence, and were in meetings with authorities and lawyers to get them witness protection. Believe it or not, they had to go. They were such disappointments, but their death meant my brother didn't get a chance to. It worked out for me, even if I did lose two good people out of it. Well, I can't call them good people now. Bastards were going to turn me in. No one turns Master in." Andrew laughed. He really did enjoy the Master persona. At first, he'd not wanted to believe that Rebecca and Jeff could turn on him, but when all the evidence had been mounting, he didn't have a choice. At least Gash didn't get to have his revenge, and he got a little pleasure out of that. He'd always, even growing up, loved to take shit away from Gash. Soon, he was going to take Charlotte, and then the club, and finally, only when he was ready, would he take Gash's life. He wanted to make his brother bleed first.

Russell moved to stand beside him.

Andrew loved the finer things in life, and he'd worked his way into an old woman's heart, taking her money, her business. For ten years he'd worked his way so that he had the money he needed at his disposal. He had the means to stay off the radar, and to tempt people to do whatever the fuck he wanted, and he did it because he loved it. Everything was a game, and everyone had a price. Andrew loved to find out what it was that made everyone tick, and what he could do in order to make them suffer. God, he loved making them suffer.

"You're not invincible," Russell said.

He turned toward the two women who were chained together in his room. Paris, she was bleeding from the beating that he'd given her. Her sister, she was simply dazed. He was waiting for the call from the hospital to let him know that Spider was awake. Once he was awake, he'd send the sister, and keep Paris to himself. If Spider died, he'd send the sister back to Chaos Bleeds, only she'd be dead as well.

His job was fun. "No one is going to capture us, Russell. We're not going to die. You see, the one thing I learned making my way to the top, is you can't take someone out who doesn't have a conscience. I don't care if I kill a woman, take what I want, and she's screaming as I do it. I've killed without a care. That's why I will come out of this alive. The Skulls and Chaos Bleeds, they care. They have people they care about, and that will be their downfall. Devil has kids, and I can happily pull the trigger. Bang, bang, bang, and his kids are dead."

Russell sighed. "What do you want me to do?"

"Go and see Angel's doctor. Find out everything you can, and let's see what we can do to start bringing down The Skulls. Everyone knows Lash loves his woman. I'd like to see what he'd do when I take her out of the picture. Pregnant women get so sick at times."

His friend nodded and left.

He had a plan, and a game to play, and Andrew intended to enjoy every single second of it.

Chapter Fifteen

Gash stared around the clubhouse, which had been decorated for his wedding. It had been a couple of days since Charlotte was taken, and the revelation that Andrew was Master. Whizz had gotten the file on everything Andre had been involved in. There was no point him hiding his identity anymore as they all knew. He'd been growing from strength to strength ever since Tiny kicked him out of The Skulls.

Ned Walker, Eva's father, had arrived at the clubhouse the day after, and together they had started to go through the file. Ned wasn't happy as it had shown that he had some business dealings with Andrew.

"I brought this fucker close to you," Ned said. "I'm going to fucking kill him. He put my little girl at risk."

It had taken Eva and his grandchildren to calm him down.

Devil had called to say that he wouldn't be arriving at the end of the week. Spider had woken up from his coma, and Paris's sister had been delivered to the Chaos Bleeds clubhouse. She had been beaten, and after today, The Skulls were going to open their club to the Chaos Bleeds crew. The Skulls were going to Piston County to offer extra protection for the journey back to Fort Wills. It was the first time The Skulls were leaving Fort Wills, but Lash had called on The Skulls' nomad chapter, with Twisted, Adam, and Happy helping to get the brothers into town.

"Are you okay?" Tiny asked.

Gash turned to see his ex-Prez standing beside him.

"Yes."

"I'm sorry," Tony said.

Gash frowned. "Why are you sorry?"

"I shouldn't have let Andrew go. He's your brother—"

"Andrew made his choice, and there's nothing you or I could have done. That fucker has it coming to him, and now we know what the hell is going on, we're going to fight him. I'm not going to give up, and neither should you. I don't blame you. Andrew, he's not my brother." He touched Tiny's shoulder. "There's no one to blame here."

They shared a moment, and Tiny nodded. "You think you're ready to be a husband."

"I should have been a husband years ago. I'm making up for lost time."

Just then, music started playing, and he turned to find Charlotte at the stairs. Lash had offered to give her away to him, and all of the club was present. Gash saw her dressed in a white summer dress, not a wedding dress, smiling toward him. One day when they had time, he was going to let her plan her perfect wedding. They didn't have the time to prepare for a lavish wedding now.

Once they were married, they were heading toward Piston County. Cars were packed, and bikes ready to make the journey. Devil had plans for them to live at his place, and several of the Chaos Bleeds brothers, too. The clubhouse was also going to be used as well.

Charlotte walked toward him, and Gash didn't have eyes for anyone else. He was in love with her, and they were going to be together for the rest of their lives.

"Are you sure about this?" he asked.

"Are you giving me an out?"

Gash shook his head. "Not really. I'll still marry you."

"Then marry me, Gash."

She took hold of his hand, and together they faced the priest who had agreed to bind them together.

Gash said his vows, promising to love and worship her. Charlotte promised him her heart, body, and soul.

When it came time to kiss his bride, he pulled her into his arms, holding her as he lowered her slowly, and taking her lips.

Wolf whistles erupted around the club, and when he pulled away, Charlotte was blushing.

"I love you, Charlotte, and I'll take care of you for the rest of my life."

She cupped his cheek. "I never thought it was possible to be this happy."

Sinking his fingers into her hair, he held her close. "We'll have a honeymoon, and when this is over, I'll get us a house, and we can start making that family."

"I'll hold you to that."

Gash had started out intending to get revenge. In the process he'd found the love of his life, and Charlotte had helped to repair his shattered soul. She made him whole, and gave him hope that one day soon they were going to be living a life he'd only ever dreamed about.

"It's time, brothers," Lash said.

Together, they headed out toward their car that had the sign "Just Married" on the back. Holding Charlotte's hand, he squeezed her tightly. Whatever they had to face, he'd do it with Charlotte by his side.

Epilogue

One week later
Fort Wills clubhouse

Spider stared around the clubhouse that was heaving with The Skulls and Chaos Bleeds. He'd just gotten out of the hospital, and they were waiting to hear from Master, or Andrew as he'd discovered he was called. Devil had forced him to go to Fort Wills. They were all going to The Skulls' clubhouse.

He couldn't stop thinking about Paris.

Celia had spoken to them about the bad man, and how the bad man kept hitting Paris. Spider had struggled throughout the whole time that Celia spoke. His woman's sister had the brand on the inside of her thigh, and he knew Paris would have it as well.

"Are you okay?" Stink asked, coming to sit beside him.

"Am I okay that the woman I was thinking of making mine is being raped and tortured by Gash's brother? Yeah, I'm peachy," Spider said, downing the shot of whiskey.

He was waiting for the stitches in his leg to be removed, and once they were he was going to hunt the fucker.

"Whizz is working to locate him. He keeps moving, but we're going to find him."

"And while we wait, he's getting people to come at us, left, right, and center. No one is safe. Gash should have fucking killed him when he had the chance," Spider, nodded at one of the club whores to fill his glass. He couldn't remember the bitch's name, and he didn't give a fuck what it was.

She filled it again, and he swallowed it down.

"Drinking isn't going to help," Stink said.

Spider turned to The Skull beside him. "How would you feel if it was Sandy, huh?" He pointed across the room at woman in question. "What would you do if she was taken, and you were waiting to be allowed to go and find her?"

Stink's jaw tensed up.

"Yeah, you know what I'm talking about. This is all bullshit. We haven't got time to be fucking around, but acting."

"You act without thought, and we'll create more death than life," Stink said.

"Are you some kind of fucking philosopher now?" Spider asked.

"No. I'm just trying to convince myself that I'd be able to handle Sandy's kidnapping better than you."

"Yeah, that's a good thought."

"What would Paris think?" Stink asked.

"What?"

"She's getting hurt, and you're sitting here drinking, wallowing in self-pity. Maybe she'd want you to man up, and get your balls back." Stink stood up. "Think about that."

Spider stared down in his empty glass, thinking about Paris, the woman he'd never even touched. He'd seen her getting naked plenty of times. Spider had wanted to be everything she wanted, to make her fall in love with him.

Gripping the glass tightly, he placed it on the counter.

"Do you want a refill?" the club whore asked.

Spider shook his head. "No."

He got to his feet, holding his crutches when a car squealed to a halt.

Turning toward the car, he saw the gun, heard the words that was shouted out.

"Master says, dodge this!"

The gun fired before any of them could draw their weapon.

They were at The Skulls' clubhouse, which was filled with men, women, and children. Simon charged at Tabitha, Lash went for Angel, Death for Bianca. All around him men charged at their women and kids to push them to the ground, and Spider jumped over the counter, pushing the club whore to the ground.

Bullets continued to rain down them, the pounding of the gun seemed to go on for minutes, but it was only a matter of seconds. Spider glanced down at the woman on the ground. She was struggling to breathe, and he saw the blood oozing out of her shirt.

"I've got you, hold on."

She coughed, choked, and died in his arms.

Screams and cries penetrated his ears, and as he stood up, he looked around the clubhouse.

Everyone was fallen, but what kicked him in the gut were the people who didn't seem to be moving.

"Simon!" Devil screamed.

"Tabitha!"

Everyone rushed to their kids, and Spider felt tears sting his eyes as he stared at the carnage before him. He didn't know the extent of the damage, as there were screams and cries everywhere. He didn't know who was alive or who was dead.

Master one, The Skulls and Chaos Bleeds zero.

The End

GASH

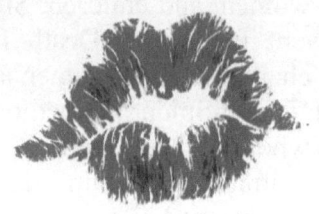

EVERNIGHT PUBLISHING ®

www.evernightpublishing.com